BEWITCHMENT AFTER THE STORM

A VIKING WITCH MYSTERY

CATE MARTIN

CHAPTER ONE

ᚺ

AUGUST HAS NEVER BEEN my favorite month of the year. Maybe that's because I've always been more of a fan of autumn than of summer. Refreshingly cool September, crisp and colorful October, November when it brings the first chill of winter but not the full arctic blast yet. Those are my favorite months.

August just feels like summer outstaying its welcome, and in the most brutal way ever.

This year was certainly no exception. The temperature had been soaring for the last nine days, a stifling heat without the slightest stirring of the air. It was cooler in my cabin in the woods than in my home inside Villmark, so I stayed there as much as I could.

But still. It might not be the only thing I missed about the modern world, but air conditioning was definitely the top one in my mind at the moment. Even a fan would be something. My rustic cabin life had neither. All I could do was pile all my red hair on top of my head and take lots of cool splashes in the water I pulled up from my well.

The hot stillness was particularly irritating to me for three main reasons.

The first, it felt cosmically unfair for the air to be so miserably humid when we were technically in a drought. The entire north shore of Lake Superior was one tinder-dry mix of wilting trees and already dead grasses and wildflowers. So why was the air itself so soaked in moisture? It was a bad distribution of resources.

The second, the oppressive stillness of the air matched my whole mood way too closely. I spent all day everyday staying as busy as I could. And given my growing responsibilities as the resident volva—the Norse variant of being a witch—to Villmark—a hidden community of descendants of a lost tribe of Norse folk from the Viking Age—staying busy wasn't even hard.

But I never managed to convince myself I was doing anything much besides waiting for Thorbjorn to return.

Thorbjorn. The tall Villmarker as comfortable in flannel and jeans as in more Viking-looking garb. With his strawberry blond hair that always got too long while he was away on patrol. With his beard that, even when traveling, he always kept neatly trimmed.

I should really ask him how he managed that sometime.

Anyway, I guess you could call him my boyfriend now, if that didn't sound so incredibly weird to say out loud. We'd been best friends when we were kids. Then I had moved away and literally forgotten ever knowing him.

Magic affects everything in my life, and not always in good ways.

I remembered all of that now, but it took a while after meeting him again for me to realize why he had always felt so familiar to me, even from the minute I thought we had first met.

In the year we'd known each other as adults, we'd spent more time apart than we had together. But I never got used to it, that being apart. In fact, it seemed to get worse every time I had to watch him head north to patrol Villmark's farthest borders, never knowing when he'd be back again.

And it was definitely worse now, when he was, I guess, kind of my boyfriend.

That just seems to be too small a word for the two of us. And yet I don't think the world has come up with a better one yet.

But anyway, the third reason the weather was bugging me was that the stifling heat was interfering with my most important duty. I was meant to be mastering all the Norse runes, one by one, in order to better understand the magic I needed to tap into as a volva.

But my current rune was Hagall. The rune of ice, among other things. My personal method for understanding the runes was to use my art to form a personal relationship with each one.

I had never felt less in touch with the spirit of ice and cold than I did that hot August.

Although, to be fair, I knew I had another hangup with this rune. It was connected in a lot of ways with the other ice rune Ur. While studying Ur, I had been staying with friends at a hunting lodge out in the forest. It had actually been cold then, back in January.

But it had also been the time of the Wild Hunt, and two sisters—Thorbjorn's cousins—had died one after another while I struggled to master Ur and use it to figure out what was going on and how to stop it.

I figured it out in the end. And justice was served.

But in my heart, I always felt like it had been one of my biggest failures since coming to Villmark. I had been so slow to fix things that time. And I had nearly lost my good friend Kara, who had been the intended third victim. I had nearly been caught by the Wild Hunt myself.

That was all hard to forget. In fact, I had been suffering a recurrence of the old nightmares the last few nights.

So I was more than a little afraid of what Hagall had in store for me.

Not that I was going to let that stop me.

But the weather wasn't helping.

The ninth day of still, hot air under hazy but not quite cloudy skies found me at my cabin in the woods with my six-toed black cat Mjolner, totally working on connecting with the Hagall rune and in no way just sitting in the yard watching the path to the north for any sign of Thorbjorn's return.

He had gone with our friend Loke as far to the north as it was possible to go. They had left a month ago. And yet, there was still no way he could be there and back so soon.

Or so I kept telling myself. Even as I kept watching that path.

The rune Hagall looks like a capital I with an X drawn on top of it. Like the most basic drawing of a snowflake, six points coming off a center.

If you connected the points with more lines to enclose the whole thing in a pentagon, you made a powerful shape that contained every other rune in one way or another.

Basically, it was an important rune with many crucial uses.

So it was almost disrespectful, the way I found myself with my sketchbook propped up on my knees just drawing snowflake after snowflake in charcoal.

I was using my thinnest willow stick. The marks it made were the finest, lightest marks I could make with charcoal.

But all I was really doing was filling a page with dark gray dust. It wasn't artful. And it wasn't making me feel any connection at all.

Waiting was one thing. But this was just wasting time.

I had filled three pages like this and was just thinking about heading inside to see if I had any iced tea left in my icebox—even though I knew the answer to that question was no; I had been too lazy to refill the pitcher when I had finished it off the night before—when Mjolner interrupted me with a single meow.

I was sitting on one of the benches around my fire pit, although it was far too hot for a fire even after dark lately. Mjolner was sitting across from me, sitting primly as he tended to do, tail wrapped neatly around his over-sized paws.

He was looking at me intently with his yellow-green eyes, and when he saw me looking back, he gave me a slow wink.

"Hello to you, too," I said, not sure if I was irritated by the interruption or not. It was a little out of character for him to meow at me when I was working.

But, to be honest, I hadn't really been working.

He meowed again, that same toneless meow that I didn't understand. I knew the particular meow he used that meant he was hungry, or the meow that meant he needed me to move over so he could sit beside me, or the shriller meow that meant someone in

Villmark or outside of it needed my help. But this was none of those.

Even as I puzzled over it, I was putting my charcoal and sketch-book away.

Something was different, more than just his meow. The air felt different.

I looked up at the sky. My cabin was in a clearing in the woods, and while I couldn't really get a glimpse of any horizon around me, I had an unimpeded view of straight up.

Nothing was different there, though. The sun was still shining white hot through the hazy layer of gray that covered the entire sky. As an artist, I didn't like the palette at all. Where was the indigo? The golden yellow? The fluffy white?

Nowhere. Not this August.

The sky was the same as it had been for the last nine days, but still I felt unsettled.

Nothing had changed, I realized. But something was *about* to.

"Come on, Mjolner," I said, snatching up my art bag and headed back inside my cabin. "We're going to head back into town."

Mjolner meowed again, but this time I understood him perfectly. He agreed with my plan wholeheartedly, although there was an undercurrent that said he wished I would hurry.

I didn't need to pack much, just the few clothes I had wanted to take back to town to wash where there was proper plumbing with hot water and everything. It only took a few seconds. Then I pulled the cabin door shut behind me, slung my duffel bag of clothes and my art bag both over my shoulder, and headed towards the path I *hadn't* been watching every day since coming to the cabin.

The one that headed south and east, back to Villmark.

It was cooler in the trees than it had been in the clearing around my cabin, but not by much. The insects were droning, but even they sounded irritated by the unrelenting heat. The path underfoot was more covered in dried leaves than usual for the summertime, and my every step crunched loudly.

Luckily, it had been quite some time since I'd had any reason to fear walking through these woods. I knew how to hide my inherent magic from the eyes of those who stalk such things. And I had senses of my own now. Anyone or anything that meant me harm couldn't possibly catch me unaware.

Not that I wasn't being alert as I walked. I paid attention to everything in the woods around me, identifying the rustle of a rabbit scurrying away from me and the snap when a deer stepped on a fallen branch.

The woods held no danger for me. Not that day.

And yet that feeling of something about to happen kept growing stronger in my mind.

Apparently in Mjolner's, too. He walked ahead of me, keeping a brisk pace that he clearly expected me to match.

I happily obliged.

The path from my cabin led to the far northern end of Villmark, at the top of a hill where a circle of trees ringed by benches stood as if marking the highest elevation of the town.

The trees' leaves were wilted, but still more green than brown. I supposed that was something.

But enough leaves had fallen from its branches that my footsteps were still punctuated with constant crunching sounds as I walked.

Then I realized the reason that crunching sounded so loud in my ears was because Villmark itself was almost entirely silent.

It was the middle of the afternoon. And yet I had never heard the place so quiet. Even in the middle of the night, there was always a dog here or there barking over something. A stray Villmarker whistling to themselves as they made their way home. A crying infant in a house with its windows opened. Something.

I stopped outside the gate that led into the garden of Valki and Gunna's house. Their five sons—collectively called the Thors by everyone save their own father—all lived in that house with their parents, although they were seldom all home at once. In fact, in the entire time I'd been in Villmark, the only time I had seen them all at home together was at the wedding for the second youngest Thor, Thorge.

Their middle son Thorbjorn was in the north with Loke, as I well knew. But where was everyone else?

Most of the others would be out on other patrols. It had been a while since I had checked in with the council, but they would be able to tell me where each had headed off to the last time they had left town, and when they had predicted they would be back.

Still, Valki had told me he preferred to keep one son home at all times, for Gunna's sake. I wasn't sure which son it was at the moment.

But the house was completely quiet. There was no sign of anyone at home.

Not that I could see much over their garden fence.

Mjolner meowed at me again, as if he sensed me debating knocking on the door to see who was home. It was an urgent sort of meow.

"What's up?" I asked him, but he just turned away from me and continued leading the way down the south slope of the hill, down to the center of Villmark. Down to my other home just off the square of the village commons.

I hoisted the straps of my two bags higher on my shoulder, then looked up at the sky again. I had a clearer view of it here than I had back at my cabin, and definitely clearer than at any point during my walk through the woods.

The gray haze was still there. But I could see the horizon now.

A storm was blowing in. I could see the darker blue-gray to steel-gray of clouds piling up on the horizon. Like that storm was pausing for a moment, staying in one place to build power before it would advance on us.

As unnerving as the sight of an approaching storm was, this one had an added twist.

Storms in Villmark nearly always come from the west, from over the hills.

But this storm was brewing to the east, over the heart of Lake Superior.

And even as I was gaping at it, I saw the exact instant where the storm unpaused. When those clouds stopped roiling in place and started galloping towards Villmark.

Towards me, standing exposed near the peak of the highest hill.

I didn't need Mjolner to tell me to hurry again. I was already jogging.

This storm was going to be a doozy. I knew that even before the first blast of wind struck me like a wall of ice, nearly knocking me off of my feet.

No wonder the town was so quiet. Every thinking person had seen those clouds forming and had gotten safely home well in time to batten down the hatches, so to speak.

Everyone but me.

I ran down the cobblestoned road, skirting the commons with its central public well, although I could hear the creaking of its bucket mechanism as it blew in the fierce wind.

I could hear the sound of rain behind me, to the east, closer to the lake. It was like hearing the steps of an advancing army, drawing in a line ever closer to where I was fumbling with the latch.

I was inside my garden when I realized what I was hearing closing in on me wasn't rain. It was hail.

Then I saw a hailstone fall right at my feet. It was somewhere between the size of a baseball and the size of a softball. Not that the distinction mattered. It was well past the size where getting hit on the head with one was going to really ruin my day.

Mjolner was yowling now, standing in what little protection the doorway of my house offered. Stupidly, but on autopilot I guess, I took the time to be sure the gate was latched behind me.

Then I ran to the door, throwing it open and spilling into the entryway with Mjolner zipping past me just before the skies really opened up.

I dropped both my bags, but that was the most movement I was capable of at that moment. I just stood there, staring at the enormous balls of hoary frost that plummeted from the sky, bouncing off the paving stones of my front garden.

This was going to cause a lot of damage. I could see a few of those paving stones cracking under the impact of the hailstones. They would need to be replaced when this storm had passed.

But I had no idea what the storm was doing to my roof. It sounded so loud, it couldn't be good.

Those clouds had been across the entire horizon. There was no way that any part of Villmark was avoiding this. Or Runde either, closer to the lake in the modern world.

There was going to be so much mess to clean up.

But the one thought I couldn't shake no matter how hard I tried was the feeling like maybe this hailstorm had been my fault. I had messed up forming the connection.

Either I had just failed to stop a bad thing again, or—the thought that really turned my blood cold—trying to connect with the rune had actually *summoned* this storm.

I hoped I was wrong.

But either way, I just didn't have any luck with ice runes.

CHAPTER TWO

THE HAIL PART of the storm only lasted for about ten minutes. But ten minutes was enough.

Especially when it was followed up by an entire night of torrential rain. The wind mostly held off, but the hot, humid air was now a cold, damp air, which was really no improvement at all.

I closed my front door when the hail stopped, but then spent more than an hour standing at the floor to ceiling windows in my living room, watching the rain fall over the expanse of Villmark I could see downhill to the south of my house.

Or as much as I could see of it. It was raining so hard that even before the sun set, it was impossible to see very far through the shimmering gray curtains of wet.

In the end, when it was too dark to see past the glass itself, I just climbed under the covers of my bed with Mjolner curled up on my pillow, his spine pressed tight against the back of my neck, and got what sleep I could.

The pounding of the rain on the roof overhead was loud, but monotonous. Once I was asleep, I slept hard.

And woke with a start when the rain stopped just as suddenly as it had started.

I got out of bed, ignoring Mjolner's usual meow of protest. That cat never wanted me to get up in the morning. But I had to take a look around. I had to see how bad the damage was.

I went back downstairs to my living room and looked out those windows again. I had an unimpeded view now, all the way to the horizon.

The sky had finally returned to its best summer indigo. The few clouds that lingered across its expanse were of the white and fluffy variety, but even those were small and well spaced from each other.

And the rising sun was a happy shade of yellow.

I could just see the lake to my left, sparkling in a thousand silver lights where the morning sun hit the always moving water. But that lake looked the same as it always did to me: cold and more than a little deadly.

To the west, the hills were shining in their own way as the drops of rain that still clung to their less than lush leaves and branches caught the rising sun. It wasn't exactly pretty, but it called to the artist in me. I knew just how I would render it in a really wet watercolor. Lots of intentional drips and washouts for effect. I almost wanted to turn away from the window and head to my easel right that moment.

But then I finally directed my attention to the village itself, and I knew I would have no time for art that day.

I could see downed tree branches and even entire trees everywhere. A lot of the rooflines were showing damage, and I saw more than a few windows that had been cracked or smashed entirely.

But I could also see Villmarkers emerging from doorways. I wasn't the only one who had been awoken by the alarm clock of no more rain. Some were already heading towards tool sheds to retrieve what would be needed to deal with the fallen trees. Others were picking up smaller branches, or sweeping detritus from the road.

But some were standing in mute shock. And those were the ones that might need my help first.

It's what my mormor—my grandmother—would do, if she were here in Villmark. I didn't have her way with people, but I had to at least try. I had to do my part.

I ran back upstairs and dressed not in my formal volva gown but in my more modern clothes: jeans and a T-shirt with a lightweight flannel shirt over it, as I suspected the cold air the storm had blown in was likely still lingering. I doubted I would be asked to do any manual labor, but I didn't want to look like I wasn't prepared for it if it was needed.

Even so, I still took my art bag with me. I never left home without it. Aside from using sketching to channel my magic, I also kept my bronze wand in its box buried deep inside that bag. I never knew when I might need one or the other.

"Are you coming?" I asked Mjolner as I perched on the end of my bed to pull on my sneakers. He opened a single eye and gave me a very baleful look, like I should've known better than to ask him such a question. "Just checking," I told him. "Do you know where I should go first?"

He meowed noncommittally then closed his eyes and resumed his nap. Clearly, he didn't think I needed any guidance from him.

As it turned out, he was right. All I had to do was step outside. The minute the first Villmarker saw me emerge from my garden gate, the word got around that I was back in town.

And everyone knew where to find me when I was in town.

In fact, a crowd was already gathering around me. All talking at once. I did my best to follow every disparate thread of speech coming my way. And honestly, I did a pretty good job considering most of them were speaking Villmarker Norse. For a language I hadn't understood a word of just a year before, I was very nearly fluent in it now.

And all the Villmarkers knew it. Although many of them spoke modern English, none of them jumped to speaking it with me without failing to get their point across in their own tongue first anymore. I took more than a little pride in that fact.

But I still felt a little out of sorts.

It always felt odd when I tried dealing with Villmarkers without either my mormor or Thorbjorn at my side. But my grandmother lived in the modern town of Runde full-time now. And Thorbjorn was, of course, still in the north.

My other most constant companion, Loke, had gone with him. And even as I bit back a laugh at the idea of antisocial Loke—Villmark's most notorious outsider—helping me deal with the needs of the community at large, I still really wished he was there.

He and I shared a common feeling that trouble was coming for Villmark. But we didn't know what form that trouble would take, or how we could protect Villmark from it. Those questions were part of why Loke had felt he had to go to the north. He was searching for a lot of answers, but those were some of the big ones.

Had this storm been the first of many troubles coming Villmark's way? Or was it just what it appeared to be, freakish but in no way supernatural weather?

I really wished Loke was there so we could argue over it.

But I had no idea when he'd be back, only that it would be long after Thorbjorn was back. And those both felt like points in the woefully distant future.

I looked around for the Mikkelsen sisters, Nilda and Kara. They would be hard to miss in a crowd, even a Villmarker crowd, looking like mythical Valkyries as they did. They had long been the first two to step up when the Thors were too busy to deal with a problem, and they had been my first teachers in the world of Villmark and its people.

Their current absence was the most puzzling, because I knew they were both in town. Kara had traveled with her new husband Thorge while he patrolled for the first month after their wedding, but she was in town without him now, home with her sister and her parents.

I had no reason to expect the two sisters to always come to me when I needed them, but still. It was weird that they hadn't. They always just seemed to know when I needed their native Villmarker point of view. And yet they weren't here now, when I needed just that.

I hoped they were all right.

I was still looking in the direction of their house, completely out of view across the many blocks between it and where I was standing, when a familiar face finally appeared at my side.

Roarr Egilsen.

And I tried really hard not to pull away from him. Because as much as Roarr had done questionable things in the first month I had known him, in the ten months since that time, he had never done anything less than strive to be helpful to me.

"Ingrid," he said with a nod as he approached me. It was not the world's most confident nod. It was almost like I could feel him bracing for me to rebuff him.

Which just made me feel worse that I had been pondering it, if only for a second.

Not that his body language ever spoke of confidence. He was tall, even for a Villmarker, nearly as tall as the Thors. But he always walked with his shoulders hunched, head down and hands in his pockets. Like he was desperately hoping not to be noticed.

So him stepping up to me now meant something. I knew it didn't come naturally to him.

And more than that, honestly, in that moment, he really *could* help me.

To start with, the minute he stepped up to speak with me, the other Villmarkers fell back, then wandered away. Like whatever Roarr needed me for, they already knew it was more important than what they had been clamoring for me to do.

But when they stepped back, it wasn't in a resentful way. They just broke off into groups to sort out how they were going to fix what they could without magic. There wouldn't be any sore feelings to be soothed later.

So I turned my full attention to Roarr.

"Roarr," I said and gave him a smile. "I hope all is well at your house?"

"Yes, we came through all right," he said, glancing back over his shoulder as if to be sure that hadn't changed in the last minute. Then he looked back at me again. "I assume you're heading down to the farms to the south. I wanted to volunteer to accompany you. Only because I know Thorbjorn and Loke are still in the north, of course."

He was blushing furiously by the time he was done speaking those words. And my puzzled frown didn't exactly put him at ease.

"The farms to the south?" I asked.

"Oh, sure," he said, nodding again. "The hail wiped out most of the crops. The council is on top of that already, planning for the shortfall this harvest. But the storm took out some of the older structures on the farms, too. But even the farms that were untouched, after a storm like that, they're going to want you to buff up their protective runes just to be on the safe side."

"Oh," I said. "Right."

That was the other side of the Hagall coin. As much as it was the rune of hail, it was also a rune of protection. Because in its enclosed hexagon form, it contained all the power of all the runes.

I had seen that form of the rune painted on all the barns and farmhouses scattered over the hills south of Villmark. I just hadn't given any thought to who had put those marks there.

But it made perfect sense the farmers hadn't done it themselves. Not when Villmark had its own volva to do such things for them.

"Mormor usually does this, right?" I said to Roarr in a whisper. Even as I said it, I knew it was a stupid question.

But he didn't seem bothered by it. He just nodded again and said, "Of course she doesn't come into town much anymore. I know they're all expecting you to do it this time."

"Every farm is waiting for me?" I asked.

"Well, yeah," he said. "Every farm."

"Every farm," I said again.

I didn't have an exact number in my head, but even an approximation told me I now knew what I'd be doing all day.

"I put myself in your hands, then," I said to him. He seemed startled at first, but then managed a crooked grin. Pleased, as always, to be of some help. "Guide me. Where to first?" I asked.

"Magna in the marketplace has the best paints," he said.

"Magna that sells wood sculptures?" I asked. I had met her once before while investigating a murder. She hadn't been a suspect, just a lead, and she'd been helpful enough. But I hadn't been back to her shop since. The cabin in the woods I had been gifted contained all the wood sculptures I could ever need.

"She works with a lot of local artists, not just wood carvers," Roarr said. "I'm surprised you two haven't mixed together more."

"I don't get out socially as much as I ought to," I admitted.

"Yeah. I hear that," he said with a whimsical sounding sigh. Like he never got out enough either. But then he was all business again. "Your grandmother always used Magna's paints when she had to retouch the protective runes. I suppose there must have been a reason."

"Then that's where we should go," I said.

We fell into step together, following the road south towards the cross street where all the markets and shops were located.

But I couldn't help sneaking glances at Roarr's face. He wasn't like Loke. He didn't have strange powers or magical insights. Or at least, not that I knew of.

But he had been in the thrall of Halldis, a woman who had never been volva but had definitely been some kind of witch. She had used him to bad ends, and to this day I still didn't know just how much he had been rigidly controlled and how much he had been just not fighting her very much.

It was a question that always plagued me. Every time I thought I knew how I felt about it, something would unsettle my mind all over again. It was a constant puzzle, whether or not I could trust him.

But it wasn't the question on my mind in that moment.

"Ingrid," he said, not looking over at me, but clearly aware that I kept looking at him.

"Sorry. I was just wondering what you thought of the storm," I said.

"What do you mean?" he asked.

"Well, you know a little about magic. Not how to use it, but what it feels like when it's… in use," I said lamely.

Halldis, as much as she had or hadn't done with Roarr himself, had briefly treated me like her own personal puppet. Under the influence of one of her spells, I had walked straight into her cottage and put myself in her power. And there hadn't been a thing I could do to fight it.

Then, I reminded myself. She had done that when I hadn't even known what I was yet. She could never do it now.

But I hated the memory of how that had felt, being entirely in her power.

"Yes. I know that feeling," Roarr said softly. "But what does that have to do with the storm?"

"It didn't feel magical to you at all?" I asked.

"Did it to you? I think that would be the more important question," he said.

"I don't know. Not for sure. That's why I'm curious about your perceptions," I said.

We walked in silence for the last stretch of block to the door of Magna's shop, but Roarr stopped there without going inside. I could see he was still in thought, so I patiently waited.

"Halldis never tried to control the weather," he said at length, his voice quieter than ever. It was almost a strain to catch his words. "Still, this didn't feel like magic to me. It just felt like a storm. But, you know, for the last nine days, it felt like it was on its way. You know?"

"I do know," I said.

Roarr just nodded as if to himself, then opened the door and disappeared into Magna's shop.

I cast one last glance up at the sky, clear and blue and completely unthreatening now. Then I followed him inside.

CHAPTER THREE

I was wrong about painting protective runes on all the farm buildings in Villmark taking all day.

It actually took two days. And part of a third.

It was also far more draining than I had anticipated. Because of course it wasn't just touching up the paint on the bind runes that were already on the buildings. That was the easy part.

But it didn't mean anything if I wasn't channeling my volva power into the rune I was painting. The rune that was all runes.

It was a lot.

Every time I did it, it left me feeling shaking and drained. And when I was done, I had to follow Roarr to the next farm and do it all over again.

But few things I had done since coming to Villmark had made me feel more like I really was a volva. When I focused on the runes and their power and put that focus into my painting, I could feel in a concrete way the protective magic I was creating.

That was really cool.

But also I could see the faint hints of other, older paint under the Hagall bind runes my grandmother had painted decades before. I touched a bit of blue paint that had nearly faded back to the color of the wood beneath it, and I sensed the woman I had met once briefly when I had found myself back in the Villmark of the 1930s.

My great-great-grandmother had painted that one.

And it wasn't even the oldest. Some of the farmhouses were more than two centuries old. Nothing went all the way back to our founder Torfa's time, of course. Nothing was as old as the ancestral fire we kept always burning in the cave behind the waterfall that marked the boundary between Villmark and Runde, although the well in the center of the village was almost as old. But these farmhouses were still older than most places I'd been in Minnesota.

As tired as I was, feeling that connection to the past kind of charged me at the same time.

More than that, I met a lot of people those three days that I had never met before. The farmers who lived south of the village proper were busy folk who didn't go into town for more than the occasional shopping trip. And I had never been more than a reluctant shopper myself. To the point where I often tried to find ways to convince Nilda or Kara to pick up groceries for me. More than I really ought to.

Despite the relatively small size of the community, there was still a distinctively different sound to the way the farmers spoke Villmarker Norse compared to the villagers. So, in a way, I was grateful I hadn't mingled with them before. I had a better grasp of the language now. And that mattered to them.

It was nice to see one after another faces shift from cautious aloofness to grudging respect when they found I could converse with them, even if I stumbled over a few of their more unique phrasings.

All in all, it had been a good handful of days. I didn't even mind that much that Roarr had been my only constant company the entire time.

Mjolner's naps were keeping him indoors.

And Thorbjorn and Loke were still in the north.

I did spare a few moments to worry why I hadn't seen or heard from Nilda and Kara. But the days had been long, and when I was finally stumbling back into town to sleep until it was time to take up the work again, I honestly never remembered to check in with them. I just crashed face-first into my pillow, ignoring Mjolner's meowing protests, and slipped into the black oblivion of exhausted sleep.

Then, on the third day, I finally finished the last protective rune on the last house. I was done. There was no more work to be done.

"I feel like I'm still tingling," I said to Roarr, looking down at my own hands. They were spattered with paint, but there was no visible sign of the little arcs of electricity that I could still feel jumping from fingertip to fingertip. Residual magic power.

"Do you need to ground yourself or something?" he asked, looking down at my hands as if he could also see what I was feeling.

"I don't think so," I said. Then I grinned at him. "Look at you, with the electrical lingo."

"I've helped Andrew's grandfather repair automobiles before," he said. Which was definitely news to me.

"You have?"

"Two years ago, all summer," he said.

He sounded so sad when he said it, and his body slouched in on itself even more powerfully than it already was.

"Oh. Right," I said, guessing what he was leaving unsaid.

He had been in love with a Runde girl. She had since died. Or rather, was murdered. Pretty much the moment I had come to town, actually. My arrival had been dramatic in a lot of ways.

But he had been in love with her for years at that point. They had gotten past the puppy love stage to actually talking about what their future together would look like.

I knew he had planned to leave Villmark and live in the modern world with her. The part I had never thought through before was that, of course, he'd need job skills that translated to that world.

Also paperwork that proved he existed. But the job skills were probably easier for him to come by first.

"How did you like it?" I asked him as I picked up my art bag. He was already a few steps ahead of me, following the path from the farm to the main road that wound its way around cow-dotted hillsides to the south end of Villmark.

"Fixing cars? It was interesting," he said, slowing his pace until I could catch up with him. "Not much use for it here, of course."

"A few of these farmers have old trucks," I said.

"They do," he agreed. But he said no more.

"It's been almost a year," I said to him.

"Sometimes it feels like yesterday. Sometimes it feels like a thousand years ago," he said. Then he fell silent again.

I took a breath and plunged in once more. "I'm not talking about your grief process, you know. I've lost both of my parents. I know that isn't a straight line. Saying it's been a year when you're talking about grief, it almost doesn't mean anything at all."

"Then what *do* you mean?" he asked. He glanced over, not so much at me but at least at my feet.

"I mean your life. You've been on pause for as long as I've known you. But I think it's time for you to decide what you're going to do... Well, not with your life. That's too big. But what you're going to do next, anyway. Decide, and then start taking a few steps. It doesn't have to be fixing cars. But it could be, if you want it to," I added as an afterthought, and gave him what I hoped was a disarming grin.

"I understand you," he said, in that slow way he often spoke. Like each word he uttered had been carefully chosen.

"Okay," I said, giving in. He wasn't ready to have this conversation. That was fine. "If you ever need a sounding board for your thoughts, though, I'm here."

His lips moved, and I realized he was repeating my last words. His English was more fluent than my Villmarker Norse, so I knew he understood me. But he was listening the same way he spoke, considering each word's meaning carefully.

Which was almost embarrassing. I had just been *talking*, not orating.

But before I could stammer out an explanation or worse yet an apology, I saw the crooked grin all but hidden under the bend of his head as he watched the road before us.

"I will remember that, Ingrid," he said. "Sounding board."

We had reached the edge of town. I had expected we'd walk

together to the commons in the center of town, since his home was to the left on the main east-west road that crossed the north-south one we were walking there. But after he had spoken those words, he raised a hand in silent farewell, then disappeared among the sparse crowds that were milling near the public gardens.

No one that tall should be able to disappear into a crowd that fast.

But I had said my piece. I couldn't blame him for not exactly needing my guidance. As strong as my volva powers were becoming, I still couldn't hold a candle to my grandmother in the arena of wise counsel.

Luckily, as she opened her mead hall every night at sunset and hosted all comers, whether from Villmark or Runde, to drink her mead and eat her roasted meats, she was still available for anyone who needed her advice on any matter at all.

But I was her granddaughter. And if that came with any benefit at all, it was that I didn't have to wait for the mead hall to open at sunset to get a moment of her time.

So I walked on past my own garden gate, turned right at the commons, and followed the eastern road out of town. I left the cobblestones behind as the road became a dirt path that drew a more or less straight line from the edge of town through a stand of birch trees to the high meadow that overlooked Runde and Lake Superior beyond.

The hail damage wasn't so bad out on the meadow, but only because the drought had already baked off most of the grasses and wildflowers I was accustomed to seeing here. There was a bit of summer left, but I doubted it would be enough for any of those plants to recover. They would just gather their resources to survive the coming winter and make a finer show in the spring.

Or so I hoped. The changing of the seasons so far north and on the shore of the cold waters of Lake Superior was something I was still getting used to.

I walked out to the edge of the meadow to the top of the rocky bluff. I could see the top of the waterfall off to my right and feel its cool spray when the random gusts of wind hit me just right.

The lake looked as outwardly sparkling as ever. The last three days had all been sunny and warm but not hot or humid, a welcome reprieve I doubted would last as long as the bad weather had held out for.

Runde directly below me was harder to make out. The homes the fishing people of Runde lived in clustered closer to the shore and were hidden from my view by the tall evergreen trees.

The homes of the farming people of Runde were mostly on the south side of the river, not quite in range of my sight on this side of the waterfall.

But I could see the mead hall almost at my feet, untouched by hail. The spells my grandmother wove to protect that place were more about preventing it and its magic from being discovered by outsiders who might pass through Runde for whatever reason. But protection from the elements like hail was so basic, I had just spent the last three days creating it for buildings of much less value to the community than my grandmother's mead hall.

I left the view behind, finding the outline of jutting stone in the middle of the grassy meadow. Those boulders marked the place where the complex of caves behind the waterfall sent one winding passage up to the open air.

I followed it, climbing down a mostly natural staircase into the central chamber where several tunnels met. There was no electricity in these caves, but the light from the ancestral fire was visible even before the sunlight from behind me completely died away. And I had been through these caves so many times I could find my way blindfolded if I needed to.

I felt a strange stab of disappointment when I found Valki waiting alone by the ancestral fire. I hadn't realized it, but I had been hoping to find either Nilda or Kara or preferably both on fire-tending duty.

After I spoke with my grandmother, I was definitely going to have to pay a call on their house next.

"Well met, Ingrid," Valki said, sparing me a glance from where he sat on a three-legged stool close to the flames. He was sharpening a dagger in slow, steady strokes against a whetstone, a relaxing sort of noise. I guessed he must like either the noise or the repetitive motion, because there was no way his weapons ever needed as much sharpening as he was always administering to them.

"Well met, Valki," I said. "Any news?"

I wasn't really asking about his son Thorbjorn, or even about the Mikkelsen sisters. As one of the three members of the council, Valki knew pretty much everything that happened in Villmark. And we both knew I had missed the last few council meetings.

"Only much thanks for the work you've done since the storm," he said, not looking up from the motion of his dagger. "We have a collection of gifts for you at the council longhouse."

"Gifts?" I repeated.

"The customary way for the people of Villmark to show their appreciation," he said, cocking an eyebrow in amusement, but still without looking up from his work. "Most of it is edible in one form or another, so Haraldr suggested we have someone deliver it to your house."

"That would be lovely," I said.

"The only question is, the house in town or the house in the woods?"

Then he did look up at me. The shadows on his face from the uncertain firelight made his blue eyes look suddenly dark, too dark to read. But I was pretty sure he was teasing me.

Pretty sure. But not one hundred percent.

"I'm in town at the moment," I said at last. "I don't have any plans beyond sleeping in tomorrow."

He scoffed, but his eyes were back on his work again. "As if you ever sleep in," he said under his breath.

Hey. Sometimes I did.

But not often. He had me there.

"I'm going down to Runde to see my grandmother," I told him, gesturing pointlessly towards the open cavern door we both knew I was about to walk through.

"Give her my regards," he said, throwing another momentary

glance my way. "I never get down to the mead hall as often as I would like."

"I will tell her you said hello," I said, a little flustered again.

I would've sworn that none of the council members ever went down to the mead hall on general principle. I mean, I had seen them there before, but only on what felt like official council business. I never saw a one of them drinking ale and sharing stories with the people of Runde or even the other Villmarkers that frequented the place.

Which was half of Villmark.

I ducked through the cavern door and followed the tunnel to the larger cavern behind the waterfall. This space was always cold and damp, and even in the brightest light of day tended to be treacherously dark.

But on the far side was the path that led down the bluff to Runde itself. The path was narrow, and so steep I had to use my hands nearly as often as my feet to make my way down. And I was even closer to the waterfall here than I had been in the meadow above. The wind didn't have to be all that random to spray me in cold mist here. Or to wet the rocks to trip-hazard slipperiness.

I took my time, then sped up to a jog as I reached the flat part of the path. It followed the curve of the river through parched but still tall grass, ending at the patio that stood behind the mead hall.

But it was the middle of the afternoon. I wasn't going to find my grandmother inside there.

I would have to catch her in her mobile home parked at the far end of the parking lot on the Runde side of the building that looked like a mead hall where I was now, but would look like any small town's municipal building on the far side.

As I crossed the parking lot, I looked past my grandmother's mobile home. Not because I didn't like that structure—although in fact I didn't—but because I wanted to see how far the construction was coming along on her cabin beyond it.

At a glance, it looked nearly done. The walls were up, the glass was in the windows, the stone chimney stood tall and ready to start streaming out smoke at a moment's notice.

Workers were up on the roof, finishing off the last of the roofing. I was just wondering whether they had to redo any of it because of hail damage when something else caught my eye.

Two people were walking past the cabin, hand in hand. Walking very close to each other, occasionally looking up at the gorgeous sky, but mostly looking at each other.

It was my two friends, Andrew and Jessica. Andrew and I had almost been an item, for like half a second. And Jessica, who owned the café off the highway, was my biggest customer in my life as an artist and illustrator. They were a couple now, which shouldn't make me feel weird, and yet it still did.

As close as they'd seemed at Kara's wedding when they'd been dancing together, they were even closer now.

Their backs were to me, but that was just as well. I hadn't been prepared to see the two of them. And I hated the jealous pang that clenched my heart. Not that I could help it.

It wasn't like I was jealous that Jessica was with Andrew. When I had decided my life had to be lived in Villmark, I had pretty much also decided that a future with Andrew wasn't ever going to happen for me. And that was fine.

No, my jealous pang was that they probably got to do this every day. Taking walks together at lunchtime. They probably took another moonlit walk after dinner, too. They could spend every minute of every day together if they wanted.

Which wasn't exactly fair of me. I knew they both had busy lives, too. Jessica worked long hours in her café, and Andrew spent as much time on his woodworking as he did helping his grandfather out with his garage and working as an EMT. It was like he had three full-time jobs.

Still. This little walk together was more time than I had had with Thorbjorn in far too long.

I took a deep breath and forced myself to look away from the two of them. I focused instead on my grandmother's door.

That stupid lightweight door that banged against the side of her mobile home no matter how hard I tried to keep a hold on the handle.

But that problem would be solved soon enough. The cabin would be ready soon. It just had to be.

As much as my grandmother's magic was grounded in her mead hall, she still deserved a home to rest in that grounded her just as much.

And I wasn't just saying that because I'd destroyed her last one. With magic.

Although I doubted that guilty feeling in my heart would ever ease until I saw her settled again with the warm wood tones of heavy timbers carved with Nordic patterns all around her, in a home smelling of a merrily crackling fire and waffles, her sturdy boots and walking stick always standing ready by the kitchen door.

CHAPTER FOUR

ᚺ

WHEN I WENT inside the mobile home, I found my grandmother standing in the tiny kitchen, gazing out the window over the sink as she held a cup of coffee in her hands. Judging from the fullness of the cup and the amount of steam rising from its surface, she had just poured it as I had walked up to her door. Since the window she was looking out of faced the parking lot and the meeting hall beyond, she must have seen me approach.

But she didn't turn to greet me when I came in. Too distracted, I guessed.

She was looking stronger every time I saw her these days. Her face had more color to it, her eyes were brighter. Even the long gray hair she always wore in a single braid down her back looked thicker and more lustrous.

It had been a little touch and go at first after her convalescence, when we'd cast the spells together to bring the mead hall back to life. But once we had all that complex magic under control, she had flourished just as much as that place had. Every night, her hall was filled with merry drinkers and storytellers from both of the worlds she loved so dearly. And she thrived on playing host to all of it.

But in this particular moment, with her attention focused not on me but on something out of that window, she looked a little pensive. Not tired exactly, just… preoccupied.

I dumped my art bag on the end of the faded couch under the front window and stretched my back. Like just the sight of that couch was enough to bring back the sense memory of too many nights spent sitting on that couch, not quite sleeping, that time two months before when Loke and I had found ourselves basically locked out of Villmark.

Not happy memories.

And all the little touches my grandmother had added to the trashy furniture that had come with her temporary home only made me feel that much worse about my role in her current homeless state. She had done her best to make this place her own, but in my eyes, adding handcrafted pillows and throws only made the old, cheaply made furniture look that much sadder.

At least the smell was clean. The recliner in the corner in particular looked like it should have a mildew smell. But even without a cabin of her own, my grandmother had imbued the place with her usual scent.

By which I mean waffles. The whole mobile home smelled like waffles. Not strongly, but persistently. Like she'd made a breakfast feast not that morning, but maybe the day before.

It wasn't until I was in the kitchen itself that the smell of the just brewed coffee finally overwhelmed that waffle smell.

"Help yourself," my grandmother told me without turning away from the window. She brought her own cup closer to her mouth but moved it away again without quite taking a sip.

"A little late in the day for me to be having caffeine," I said. Especially since, despite the number of things I had to do first, the one thing I was really looking forward to doing was collapsing on my bed and sleeping for at least ten hours. More if I could manage it.

My grandmother just shrugged. I had lived with her enough over the last year to remember how coffee was an anytime beverage for her. It never seemed to bother her sleep schedule at all.

I guessed I had missed inheriting that gene.

"You recharged all the protective runes, I hear," she said as she finally turned away from the window to lean back against the sink counter.

"It seemed like a job I could handle on my own," I said.

"You figured I had my hands full just maintaining the mead hall," she said. I couldn't quite tell if she was annoyed about that or was teasing me.

My grandmother was the master of tone. She knew when she said those words, I wouldn't be able to tell which way she meant them.

"I thought it would be a good experience for me doing something everyone in the village could see," I said, trying not to sound defensive.

Alas, I wasn't a master of my tone. Or of my facial coloring, which tended to flush red and let everyone know when I was having feelings.

"You're not wrong about that," she said and finally took a sip of her coffee. "I'm glad I stayed out of it."

"Were you planning on coming up to help?" I asked.

"If you asked," she said. But there was a twinkle in her eye that I knew well.

"If I didn't ask but needed help, you'd've been there," I said.

She just shrugged and took another sip of coffee.

But I already knew she'd always be there if I needed her. If she didn't sense it herself when I got in over my head, Mjolner always knew. And Mjolner was persistent when fetching help for me.

Very persistent.

Still, something else was nagging at me now.

"What were you looking at just now? Out the window?" I asked.

I knew it hadn't been the parking lot, and I didn't think it was the meeting hall either. That place might be her chief domain now, but it wasn't one she had any worry about taking care of. But there had been a hint of worry to her brow when she'd been looking out that window, not drinking her coffee.

"Nothing in particular," she said.

"Was it the sky?" I asked. I leaned past her to look out the window myself. The waterfall was out of sight behind the trees that lined the river banks, but the top of the bluff was just visible under the indigo skies.

"The storm has passed," she said. "It's not coming back."

"Did you feel something magic in that storm?" I asked her.

"Did you?" she countered.

"I don't know," I admitted. "I wish Loke were here."

"You don't need his confirmation to trust your own feelings, do you?" she asked.

"No," I said. Although that was kind of a lie. I mean, I preferred to have his confirmation on things. It helped to know I wasn't imagining things. "Roarr said he didn't feel like it was magical."

"We're trusting Roarr's feelings now?" she asked, cocking an eyebrow at me.

"Kara has been busy," I said. I was pretty sure my cheeks were redder than ever now.

"Roarr has his uses," my grandmother said, very grudgingly.

"He's helped me with my work for the last three days," I said.

"I know. He means well." She looked down at the coffee cup in her hands as if surprised to find it empty, then moved over to the coffeemaker to refill it. "He is more sensitive than most to the flow of magic around us all. But he's absolutely not reliable with what he infers about what he senses." Then she looked at me, her eyes intent on mine. "You know as well as I how capable he is of choosing the wrong path."

"I wasn't asking his advice. I just wondered if he felt anything," I said. "Anyway, you never answered my question. Did you sense anything about that storm?"

"If I had, do you really think I'd have waited three days for you to come ask me about it?" she asked.

Fair enough. But she was uniquely grumpy for no reason I could discern.

Then she sighed, as if she'd just realized the same thing about herself. She set her coffee cup aside, then folded her arms before giving me a more considering look. "The magical storms you've been having premonitions of, they all come from the north? Don't they?"

"Yeah," I admitted. I had forgotten that little detail. "But coming from over the lake is its own kind of weird."

She shrugged. "It happens."

"There's something in that lake I don't like," I said.

"You're not wrong to fear it. It's filled with the remains of those who didn't fear it enough," she said. "But sometimes a hailstorm is just a hailstorm. Even one as damaging as this one."

"I suppose," I said. But I wasn't comforted.

"If it's drawn you closer to the community you're looking to pledge your service to, that's a good thing," she added.

I just nodded.

She picked up her coffee cup again, looked into it, then set it aside once more with another sigh.

"You seem out of sorts," I said.

"I am, but only for the most mundane of reasons," she said. At my blank look, she laughed under her breath, then said, "Contractors."

"Oh. I suppose the hail set them back a bit on your cabin," I said.

"It only *starts* with the hail," she said. But then she waved a dismissive hand at me. "Never mind. If it were a problem magic could solve, I would've done it already. You're worried because this hailstorm blew up while you were focusing on the rune for hail. Perfectly natural. But sometimes things really are just a coincidence."

"But sometimes they aren't," I said. Although I was more than a little impressed that she had known why I was there without me even pussy-footing my way around to the topic.

"Go talk to Haraldr," she said.

"He'll put my mind at ease?" I asked skeptically.

"He's better than I am at getting you to do that for yourself," she said. I was about to argue, but she cut me off by adding, "At least, in my current state, he's your better bet."

"Are you sure I can't help?" I asked.

"I already have Andrew's assistance. More than I need, but don't tell him I said so," she said.

I nodded, but felt my face flushing yet again.

It wasn't like I ever talked to Andrew these days. A few exchanges on the group text we shared with Michelle and Jessica aside.

"Go see Haraldr," she said, all but shooing me out of her kitchen. "Then get some sleep. I can see plain as day you've been overdoing it. Nothing that a day of rest won't take care of, but be sure you take it. Grandmother's orders."

"Yes, Mormor," I said, grabbing my art bag before heading out the door.

But the minute my feet hit the pavement, I was turning back to catch her just before she could close the door behind me.

"It was hot and still for nine days before the storm," I said. "Nine days precisely."

"Nine is a number that always announces itself in all caps, bold, with lots of exclamation points," she said. "But sometimes it's still just a number."

"You didn't feel anything off at all?" I pressed one last time.

"Not a thing," she said.

I was all the way back to Villmark before I realized she had never quite answered my question.

Just what had she been looking at out her window when I'd arrived? If it had been the state of her cabin that was worrying her, why wasn't she standing in her living room looking out the window that actually offered a view across the street to where that structure was being built?

But that was the thing with my grandmother. She always had her secrets. As much as she taught me—and she had taught me so much—there were still things she didn't share. And she never invited prying.

For the second time that day, I took the main road south towards the downhill end of town. But this time I turned before the public gardens at the edge of town, walking past the tallest building in the village—the council meeting hall—to the garden gate of the oldest member of the council, my mentor, Haraldr.

I let myself in the gate, walked across his neatly swept patio, and knocked on his door.

And I hoped my grandmother was right. Because I really needed help putting my mind at ease.

CHAPTER FIVE

ᚺ

I HAD JUST RAISED my hand to knock on the door a second time when it opened up so suddenly I found myself stumbling back. Not that I was in any danger of it hitting me. Like most front doors, it opened inward.

As startling as that was, my surprise only deepened when I saw it was Haraldr himself who was on the other side of the door.

For his part, he looked as surprised to see me there as I was. Although, given the way his sparse gray hair always floated in a halo around his sun-damaged scalp and the way his eyebrows jutted out in all the directions at once, he always looked like he was at least mildly startled.

"Haraldr," I said, pulling myself together first. "I hadn't even knocked yet. And I was expecting Fulla."

Fulla was Haraldr's live-in helper, a teenage girl who had been orphaned at a young age with no siblings, no other close family. She had been placed with Haraldr so the two of them could look out for each other. She was a hard worker and took excellent care of Haraldr, although I often worried that she might be working a little too hard for a girl her age.

"Fulla is out for the afternoon with a friend," he told me as he adjusted a wool wrap that was starting to slide from his shoulders. "I was about to cross the street to take a turn in the gardens. Would you like to accompany me?"

"Gladly," I said.

Apparently, my conversation with the other council member Brigida about getting Fulla a little more help had yielded fruit, and I hadn't even realized it.

Well, I had been missing a lot of meetings lately.

I waited for Haraldr to fetch his walking stick from the corner of his mud room. He gave his wrap one last tug up closer around his neck, then stepped outside, pulling the door closed behind him. Then he gave me a little smile before taking my arm so I could help him down the steps to his paved patio.

"It's a bit soon for our next lesson. Unless you felt like the recent storm showed you all you needed to know about Hagall?" he said, shooting me a twinkling look.

"Not so much the storm as the magic I've done since, reinforcing the protective runes on all the farms south of the village," I said.

"Yes, I heard," he said as we stepped out into the cobblestoned street. I pulled the gate closed behind us, then we crossed the street to the public garden on the other side.

The trees here were looking greener than the ones around my cabin, but then these were constantly tended by an entire team of gardeners. I could see the first signs of apples and pears nestled among those leaves. Despite the drought, it looked like it was going to be a good harvest this autumn.

"Before the storm, I wasn't feeling much of a connection at all," I admitted once we had chosen a path through the garden and started our walk.

"Too preoccupied by other matters?" he asked. His teasing tone was reminding me yet again of how many meetings I had missed, always choosing to stay closer to my cabin in the woods. Closer to the path to the north.

"Something like that," I said. But then I realized I wasn't being entirely fair to myself. "But not just that. It's different, this rune."

"It is," he conceded with a nod. "The first eight runes, what we call the first aett, they tell our creation story. Those are the old stories, the most retold. Not the easiest concepts, necessarily, but perhaps the most familiar."

"So it's not just Hagall? All the runes now are going to be… different?" I asked.

"Oh, well, they have their own relationship to each other," he said, giving his walking stick a jaunty little swing as he stepped. He seemed in high spirits. But then again, everyone in town was, now that the weather had finally broken. Any excuse to be outside when the sun was warm, but the air wasn't stifling hot was a good one.

"I guess I see how this one is protective now," I said. "I've been thinking about it every time I paint it. It's just solid, isn't it? It has a structure that feels perfect. Complete, maybe."

"Hmm," he said. But he said no more, waiting for me to go on.

"Right," I sighed. "How weird is this aett going to get?"

"Well, we're moving into the world of the Norns now," he said. "These are forces outside of human control. Like orlog."

"You mean like fate?" I asked.

"Meh," he said. "Not exactly. The Norns aren't like the Fates as others know them. They don't weave a tapestry that foretells all. But they create the laws that direct what will happen."

"It kind of sounds like the same thing," I said.

"Does it?" he said. There was that twinkle back in his eye, and yet his words had a real challenge in them.

"I guess I have more work to do on this one," I said. "But all I'm getting is like a snowstorm of randomness."

He chuckled at that, and I tried not to get annoyed.

"I'm serious," I said.

"I know," he said. "It's a lovely metaphor for the situation, isn't it?"

Right. Couldn't get a signal through the noise. That's what I was drawing. Literally.

"Yes. Lovely metaphor," I said drily.

"I would recommend you keep at it," he said, giving my hand on his arm a reassuring pat. "This is going to be a tough one for you."

"Why?" I asked. I mean, I had my own theories. But I was curious what his were.

"The Wild Hunt," he said, and I was so startled I actually stopped walking. It was like my legs had gone numb.

"I thought I was being silly, worrying about that," I said. I could barely manage more than a whisper. As if speaking too loudly would summon that ghostly troop once more. They had taken away two of my friends. They had nearly taken Kara.

Kara, whom I hadn't seen in too many days.

"I think I have to go," I said to him.

"Yes, but wait a moment," he said, tightening his grip on my hand as if he thought I was about to flee.

Which I kind of thought I was about to, too.

"I didn't mean Odin's Wild Hunt," he said. "There is another, you know. It's called the Wild Hunt of Holda. But it won't manifest the way the other did."

"How will it manifest?" I asked.

And, maddeningly, he just shrugged. "The lore on this is much sparser than the other. But that's so often the case with these sorts of things. Representations of dark feminine power, I mean. Personally, I think my scholar ancestors let their fear of such things get the better of them. Could it possibly be a greater peril than Odin's Wild Hunt?"

I didn't know what to say. I wanted to say no. Those nights hiding inside the safety of the hunting lodge while the Wild Hunt circled in the snow all around us… I was never going to forget those nights.

And the night I had been caught out, and found the Wild Hunt riding on my very heels, that had been the worst night of all.

I wanted to say no, nothing could be worse than that.

But I couldn't get the word out. I was too afraid I would be wrong.

"I should be looking out for a dark feminine power," I said.

"I'm not sure anyone is in any danger," he said, blinking up at the sky. I could see why he said that. What danger could possibly be closing in on such a lovely day? It was practically unthinkable.

But I could think the unthinkable, more than I liked to.

And I couldn't ignore the fact that the greatest threats to the people of Villmark had always come in the guise of women. Every single time.

"Dark doesn't necessarily equate to evil, Ingrid," Haraldr said, as if reading all my thoughts on my face. Which he probably was. "Something can be outside the light without being malevolent. Not all secrets are harmful. And certainly just because a thing is unknown to us doesn't make it an enemy."

"I understand," I said. "Still. I think my focus was in the wrong place."

"Then I'm glad we had this conversation," he said with a smile. "Where are you off to now?"

I wanted to say I was going to find Kara, to be sure she was all right. She was so much on my mind, and I needed to understand why I was fearing for her particularly. I trusted my instincts, but I liked to have a little more explanation than just having a feeling.

But the word that came out of my mouth instead was, "South."

"South?" Haraldr repeated.

I supposed we both looked a little comical, gaping at each other in surprise. That was sort of the tone of the whole afternoon for us.

But then I knew why I had said that word. "I need to figure out something about that storm. As hard as it hit Villmark proper, its focus was really south of the village. The most damage was to those farms."

"They were most vulnerable," Haraldr said. "The protective runes should've been renewed years ago. It's one of many tasks that have been left undone for too long."

He spoke those words carefully, but I heard the admonishment of my grandmother clearly enough. She had waited too long to start handing responsibility on to another.

Not that I could blame her. She had been waiting for me to return, to remember the childhood I had forgotten, to realize what I was and the things I could do. Maybe she should've taken an apprentice in the meantime, trained some other potential volva in the necessary skills.

But I was grateful she hadn't. I couldn't imagine any other life for myself now.

Not to mention her chief potential successor had been Halldis. Who had been very far from worthy of my grandmother's tutelage.

"Well, best of luck to you. I think I'll shuffle back home and eat the dinner Fulla left for me in the icebox," Haraldr said.

"I can walk you back?" I offered, but he was already shaking his head.

"No, I'm quite capable of making it on my own. Go on, now. You have things to do."

I watched him shuffle off through the orchard of fruit trees, back towards his own garden gate.

I turned to the west, heading through the gardens to emerge on the main road that would take me to the southern farms.

Then froze in place on the cobblestones as I realized just where I was standing. Directly across the street from the narrow lane between two garden fences.

The lane that led to Halldis's cabin.

It was still there. No one had touched it, or the gardens around it. I had certainly never gone back there, not after the night she had tried to kill me. My grandmother had removed anything dangerous that Halldis had left behind after she'd been imprisoned in the caves behind the waterfall. But the cabin still stood.

I chewed at my lip, debating. But in the end, I decided that really was too dangerous.

Yes, I was trying to get in touch with dark feminine energy. And that place was soaking in it.

But it was the wrong kind of dark.

I had to pay heed to Haraldr's words. Not everything that was dark was evil. But if I tried to reach out to it in a place I knew *had* been used for evil, I was never going to be able to trust what I found.

It was smarter to stick with my original plan.

I didn't even pretend like I wasn't running when I turned my back on that lane and headed south of town. I didn't stop until I was a full three hills beyond the edge of the village.

Only then did I stop, drop cross-legged to the ground, and without taking a moment to think about anything, took out my sketchbook and started scribbling on the first page in my darkest charcoals.

I slipped into the fugue state of my magic so readily I would've been quite heartened if not for the fact that the fugue state didn't allow for any such self-awareness at all.

But it passed as quickly as it had come over me. I had covered a single page with Hagall runes. But while my other pages back at my cabin had looked like snowstorms of individual snowflakes, this one was thick and black.

So thick the charcoal was blowing over the surface of the paper in the slight breeze that danced over the hilltop. The charcoal pencil in my hand was down to a nub now, and I tossed it into the side pocket of my bag to throw away later.

Still, as unremittingly black as it looked now, I could discern the lines of the form. I hadn't just filled in the page with broad strokes. This was still an overlap of Hagall snowflakes.

It was also still a really lovely metaphor of my signal-to-noise problem. All random chaos, no real clue.

I sighed, then shut the book and put it away.

But once I had stood up, I didn't head north towards town. Instead, I headed south, towards Loke's and Esja's house.

There was no reason why anyone should be there. Loke was in the north, and Esja was in town. With Nilda and Kara, unless she'd shifted over to Sigvin Olafsson's house again. She had been splitting her time between the two households while she waited for her brother to return.

So, yeah, no reason why anyone should be there. But I headed that way just the same.

Because I was curious. I had been to every farm scattered among the hills south of the village. But Loke's and Esja's house wasn't a farm. So I hadn't checked in there.

And I was suddenly sure that had been an oversight. One I had to correct.

CHAPTER SIX

ᚺ

THE FIRST TIME I had walked south to Loke's house, it had been in the middle of December, when all the rolling hills had been covered in snow, the taller hills to the west had been a patchwork of bare-branched deciduous trees interspersed with evergreens, and cows had been scattered everywhere.

It had also been when I had just started studying the runes, making my first fumbling attempts at building a connection with their meaning and their power.

Because of the cows, I had seen the Fe rune everywhere. It had been clear as day in the pattern of the markings on every cow.

I almost chuckled at that memory. I had been dealing with a different sort of signal-to-noise problem then. Having only a superficial knowledge of the rune Fe—that it represented wealth and particularly moveable wealth like a cow—my symbol-seeing mind had conjured its form everywhere.

It's not that I was wrong to see it. It just wasn't particularly useful at that moment.

Then, as I made the turn off the main road to a narrower, dustier track that led more or less due west between a pair of taller ranges of hills, I remembered something else I had seen that day.

I had seen the Fe rune inverted in the pattern of the wood just above the front door of Loke's house.

At the time, I had dismissed it as another phantom of my overactive imagination. And then had promptly forgotten it.

But in hindsight, after months of gaining experience in such things, I had a different take on it now.

It *had* meant something. It had meant the opposite of moveable wealth. Because what Loke and his sister Esja had was the opposite of wealth. Not only were they without resources save their slowly crumbling ancestral home, that home was holding them down. Immoveable.

I was still pondering that when the house itself came into view between the last pair of hills.

The buildings of Villmark follow two patterns. Most favor a minimalist, modernist Scandinavian look, as if these people who hadn't had contact with their distant cousins back in the old world still shared a sensibility that had evolved in parallel. Most of the village followed this pattern, with square frames and large windows, every house having its own garden behind a tall fence that offered a little privacy for the occupants despite the closeness of the neighbors.

A smaller number of Villmarkers, mostly the farmers or those who lived on the western fringes of the village itself, favored a more traditional Viking style of structure. These ranged from longhouses built from solid timbers to stone-walled sod houses.

Not that there wasn't any overlap between the two. My house in the village was Scandinavian modern, but my cabin in the woods was thoroughly Viking. Even the three members of the council itself worked in the oldest of our buildings—the longhouse that was their meeting hall—but each of them had a modern structure as their personal residence.

But Loke's house? Loke's house—like Loke himself, really—didn't fit with anything else to be found in Villmark. It didn't even look like anything anyone would expect to find in Northern Minnesota. In my hometown of St. Paul, maybe in some neighborhoods, but here?

Here, a Gothic mansion complete with spire-topped towers was a total anomaly.

It had looked dour when I had first seen it on a cold, gray December day. Even the parts that weren't still showing the damage from the long-ago fire that had killed Loke's parents were sort of a smoke gray, scarcely more colorful than the wrought-iron railings, downspouts, and window frames that were as much as it had in the way of decorative elements.

It only looked gloomier now, with the backdrop of blue skies and grass slowly returning to green after the recent rain.

Maybe that was because it was empty. It certainly felt empty as I walked up to it. There was no outward sign that said no one was home, only the knowledge in my own head that Loke was in the north and Esja was in town.

And yet, it was like the sight of that building resonated like an empty echo inside my mind.

I gave my head a little shake, but the feeling persisted.

I stopped at the bottom of the porch stairs. There was no reason to go up and knock. And I didn't really want to pull one of my mormor's usual tricks and just open the door and let myself in.

But why was I here?

I looked around at the tall trees that flanked the house, then at the cows on the hillsides beyond. I could still see the Fe around them, but it wasn't screaming at me like it had before.

I squinted into the shadows under the porch roof and could still make out the inverted Fe over the door. So I hadn't dreamed that either.

I turned and sat on the bottom step, setting my art bag beside me. Then I took out my sketchbook, but I didn't turn to a blank page. Instead, I leafed through my last few days of drawings.

I had mostly been repainting the protective runes on the farm buildings all around where I was now, but that hadn't been all I was doing. I had always taken a few moments before to chat with the families, and then a few moments after to sketch the buildings before moving on to the next farm.

I had mostly filled the entire book with those drawings. I hadn't even known why I felt compelled to draw everything. But being an artist, that wasn't an urge I ever expected to have to explain to myself. I just drew.

Looking back at them now, they really were a record of the damage each farm had withstood in the storm. All the farms had been hit harder than the village itself. But some were worse than others.

I dug out a pencil and finally turned to that first blank page, sketching out a map of the hilly area south of Villmark. I consulted my sketches and my memory, marking the location of each farm and a general sense of how bad the damage had been to their structures.

My unspoken hunch became proof before my eyes. The damage grew in severity in degrees, forming a circular pattern where things were worse closer to the center.

Like a bullseye.

And I was sitting right dead center of all of it.

I got up from the porch, sketchbook still in hand, and stepped back until I could see the full view of the house again.

It always looked wrecked. That was true. But it was obvious that all that damage was old. The hailstorm, which from what I had drawn should have been at its most devastating here, had scarcely touched this house at all.

All the windows were intact. The shingles on the roof looked no worse than the last time I had seen them. Even the shrubberies under the windows and the trees at the property line appeared entirely unharmed by the storm. In dire need of a hedge trim, but unharmed.

What did that mean?

I didn't know, but I didn't like the sinking feeling it was giving me.

Now I really wanted to get back into town, not only to find Kara and make sure she was okay, but to check in on Esja, too. Did she know anything about this?

How could she? She couldn't have been out here at the time.

And yet, did she?

But I couldn't go back just yet. I sat down in the middle of the dirt path and drew the house as I saw it before me. I slipped into another little fugue state as my pencil flew over the page, so it wasn't entirely surprising that when I was done, the entire house was surrounded by a cloud of Hagall runes. Like snow falling from the sky, blowing all around the house.

But not touching it.

I went back to the porch to fetch my bag, then tucked my book and pencil away before starting the long trudge back into town.

But my mind kept going back to Esja, and to my conversation with Haraldr.

Dark feminine energy, that's what he had called the power of Hagall. I thought I knew a little about that. I had fought forces that had that vibe a few times since I had come to Villmark.

But the word "dark" felt like a misnomer to me. I mean, the women who had been the darkest in energy had all been golden-skinned, light-eyed blondes. Some of them had even pumped that up with a little glamor-invoking magic. They had practically glowed.

And yet, yeah, I'd call every one of them dark.

And Halldis, the darkest of all, had used her magic to glow the brightest of any of them.

So clearly, if I knew anything, it was that I couldn't judge such things by appearances.

And yet, my mind refused to even touch on the idea that Esja could be somehow caught up in anything that I would describe as dark feminine energy.

She didn't glow. She wasn't golden. No, she had spent most of her life battling a mysterious illness. She was still battling it, although she had more good days than bad recently.

But while she was as light-eyed and blonde as any of the women I had faced, she wasn't golden bright at all. No, she was more… washed out. Rather like the watercolors she painted in. She was too much water diluting too little pigment.

She was also the sweetest young woman I knew. She never complained, but she also refused to let her sometimes overbearing brother coddle her too much. She lived with limitations, but she lived as fully as she could within those limitations.

No, whatever had happened with her house, it hadn't been her doing.

But it might have been because of her.

Although I couldn't imagine a reason why.

As much as we had discussed his worries about Villmark itself, I knew the main reason Loke had gone north was to search for answers to his sister's problems.

I really hoped he found them. And soon.

But in the meantime, I had promised him I would look after Esja.

Neither of us had been thinking of anything remotely like what was happening when I had made that promise. But that didn't change anything for me. I was going to look out for Esja.

And if something outside of Villmark was targeting her, some being of power I didn't yet understand, I would have to step up to meet that challenge.

I really hoped I was overreacting. I hoped I would find Esja and Kara both, and everyone would be fine, and I would just look a little silly for fussing over some snowflakes on some drawings.

And not just because it was starting to feel like that goal I had for a long night's sleep was drifting out of my reach now.

CHAPTER SEVEN

ᚺ

THE SUN WAS STARTING to set over the hills to the west as I walked back into Villmark. The shops in the marketplace were closing up for the night, and groups of Villmarkers were starting to gather to head towards the various mead halls for dinner and an evening spent in good company.

I was too tired to even wish I was doing the same. But I still had a job to do.

Esja had been splitting her time between staying with Sigvin Olafsson and the Mikkelsen sisters. From what I had seen, Esja was closer friends with Sigvin. I wasn't sure if the two had bonded over a mutual missing of Loke, who while obviously being Esja's only brother was also the source of all of Sigvin's unrequited passions. It felt like an odd basis for a friendship, but the two of them really seemed to enjoy each other's company.

Still, I was pretty sure that at the moment she was staying with the Mikkelsens, so I headed to their house first. Nilda, the older of the two valkyrie-like sisters, still lived with their parents. Kara had recently married Thorge Valkisson, and often went out with him on patrol through the countryside around the village of Villmark. My grandmother had gifted them the enclosed wagon of her late friend Reginleif, a tidy little home on wheels.

But Thorge had currently taken a patrol further out than he wanted both of them to go. So he was out far to the west with one of his brothers, and Kara was staying with her parents and sister. She was also sharing the rotation of guarding the ancestral fire behind the waterfall that separated Villmark from Runde and the rest of the world.

I reached the gate to their front garden just as the lights inside the streetlamps started flickering to life. These weren't magic, of course. Few in Villmark could use magic, and I wasn't about to expend the energy to keep the whole village lit up at night.

In fact, they had once been gas lights. But a few years before I had come up from St. Paul and rediscovered my roots in this village, one of the younger set had changed out all the gas lights for more modern LEDs that ran on solar power. The lights were only just bright enough to do the job, and the lamps were kept shielded so that the light pollution was as low as possible.

Because, as much as that was what we *did* use magic for—protecting Villmark and its environs from being detected by the rest of the world, even from the sky or from space these days—any mundane effort that could take a little of the job off of magic's plate was necessary.

I let myself into the Mikkelsens' front garden, then knocked on the door. I looked around as I waited for a response. Nilda and Kara's mother kept a lovely little garden, but clearly preferred herbs to flowers. The air smelled lovely, like lavender and thyme with a hint of the mint kept sequestered in a planter in the center of the patio.

I wasn't much of a gardener myself, but I knew the need for keeping mint contained. It spread like wildfire.

I was just wondering if I should make some sort of effort to use the space in front of my own house in town to grow something useful in a container or two when I heard the sound of someone opening the door.

It was Nilda. She looked exhausted, like a young mother who

had been kept up by a colicky baby for far too many nights in a row. Her golden hair was still in its customary braids, but they were crooked, loose in some places and twisted in others as if she'd slept in them, and not restfully. I could see strands jutting out everywhere.

And the bags under her eyes were so pronounced, she looked like she'd been in a fight and gotten two black eyes for her trouble.

But when she saw it was me standing on her doorstep, her face lit up. She ran a hand over her hair as if that smoothing gesture could possibly put everything to rights. Then she swung the door open wide so I could step into the house.

"Ingrid! I'm so happy to see you," she said.

"Is something wrong? I didn't hear that you needed me," I said. "I know I've been busy, but I would've dropped almost anything if you or Kara needed my help."

"Oh, Kara and I are all right. We're just both a little beat from all the extra guard shifts lately," she said as she led the way down the darkened corridor to the brighter living room. The floor to ceiling windows offered a lovely view of the hills to the west, just visible over the tops of the neighboring houses.

Any feeling of relief her words might have given me was dashed at once when I saw Kara herself spread out on the couch. She had her shoes off and a knit throw draped over her, but she wasn't merely catching a nap. Not with that fold of wet cloth draped over her forehead. Or the bucket set carefully within easy reach.

"What's wrong?" I asked, turning to look at Nilda. I was hoping for some sign of joy, that perhaps this was a late in the day bout of morning sickness, and I was about to hear some good news.

But before Nilda could speak, Kara was sitting up on the couch, letting the cloth fall from her forehead into her hand.

"I'm all right," she said, although she looked little better than her sister. "Really, I am," she added directly to Nilda, who was hovering in a way that threatened to turn into making a fuss.

"I should've been by sooner. I've been thinking about you all through the last days, but I never followed through. I'm sure my intuition was trying to tell me something. Why didn't I listen?" I said, mostly to myself.

"It's okay, Ingrid," Kara said. She folded the cloth into a tidy little square, then set it on a coaster on the coffee table, although to my eye it looked quite dry.

"We didn't really have any idea we'd need your help until..." Nilda started to say, then looked to her sister.

"This morning, I think," Kara said, pressing a hand to her forehead as if it still ached her.

"Yes. The last few days have been odd, but nothing seemed really wrong until Kara tried to sense things. And since then..." Nilda broke off again, but this time she just collapsed into a chair as if she no longer had the energy for standing.

"I've had a bit of a rough day," Kara said with an attempt at a smile.

"Perhaps we should start at the beginning?" I suggested, and sat down on the couch next to Kara.

The sisters looked at each other for a long moment, sharing some silent communication. Then Nilda sighed and sat forward, elbows on her knees but hands just sort of dangling off her wrists.

Seriously. Every aspect of her body language was just screaming her exhaustion at me.

"It started with the hailstorm," she said. "I mean, we know that now. Up until this morning, we just thought... I don't know what we thought."

"She's had ups and downs since her brother left," Kara said softly. "We thought it was just more of that."

"So we're talking about Esja," I said.

"Yes, we're talking about Esja," Nilda said.

"I thought she was doing well, living in town. The few times I've seen her, she's seemed in very good spirits," I said.

And tried not to show how guilty I felt, about how few and far between those "times" had been.

"She puts on her best face for you," Nilda said, and Kara nodded her silent agreement.

"She does?" I asked. This was news to me.

"She looks up to you. A lot," Kara said.

"She works very hard not to let her moodiness show when you're with her. But she does get moody. Sigvin has seen it too," Nilda said.

"Are you saying Esja is depressed?" I asked. Which would be understandable, with her brother being gone and no one knowing when he'd be back.

Or if. Although I didn't like to admit it to myself, and I would never even let Esja see a hint of such dark thoughts when I was with her, but I couldn't deny it. Sometimes my worry led me to contemplating such dark outcomes.

"Sometimes it's like that," Nilda said. "I mean, that's the part that's easiest to deal with. Maybe because it's the easiest to understand?"

She ended with a questioning look to her sister. But Kara was already shaking her head.

"No. I mean, it is easiest to understand when she's just sad. But her other moods are just harder to deal with because… well, they're just harder."

"Is she bipolar?" I asked, not sure if I would have to explain that or not.

"No, nothing like that," Nilda said.

"We spoke with Signi about it a few weeks ago, and she said no," Kara said.

Signi was a Villmarker who had left Villmark decades ago to pursue a life as a psychiatrist in the modern world. She had later returned but lived in a secret community hidden in the woods northwest of Villmark, a community filled with other people who had left for the modern world and then decided to return.

But Signi still saw some Villmarkers, from time to time, always in her professional capacity. Mostly, she worked with the people deemed unsafe to be allowed to walk freely. The prisoners kept in the cells in the caves behind the waterfall.

Although in this case, I knew that the sisters had taken Esja out to the hidden village to talk to Signi in her own home.

"But they did only speak together for barely an hour on a single afternoon," Nilda said. "They seemed to get along swimmingly. But after we left Signi's cabin—before we were even out of sight of it—Esja very firmly told both of us she wouldn't go back again. No therapy for her."

"That doesn't sound like Esja," I said with a frown.

"That's what we're trying to tell you," Nilda said. "She's not quite herself, I don't think. But even when she *is* herself, that self isn't the one she shows you."

I sighed, just resisting the urge to bury my face in my hands. Or chastise both of them for not coming to me sooner.

I really wasn't going to get that early night and long sleep until midmorning I had been hoping for.

"How firmly is firmly?" I asked at last.

"That time? She was just adamant. Not violent," Nilda said.

"She's been *violent?*" I asked.

"Just the once," Kara said quickly.

"This morning," Nilda said, giving her sister a significant look.

"What happened this morning?" I asked.

They traded another look, then Nilda spoke again. "She never came home last night. We were worried. But she interpreted that as the two of us trying to control her, I guess."

"She said some things," Kara said dully. As if even the memory of the words was a thing she had to insulate her mind from.

"And she threw some things," Nilda said, gesturing over her shoulder.

I hadn't noticed it when I'd come in—as the sight of Kara had caught all my attention—but there was a definite dent in the wall behind the chair where Nilda was sitting. Like someone had thrown something heavy.

"Esja did that?" I was still having trouble reconciling the young woman I knew with the one the Mikkelsens were describing to me.

But I'd never known either of them to lie, or even to exaggerate.

"Where is she now?" I asked, leaning forward to get up from the couch.

But Kara put her hand on my knee to keep me still. "There's more I have to tell you first," she said.

"We wrestled her to the ground and pinned her down," Nilda said.

I was trying not to interrupt, but my gasp couldn't be contained.

"Yeah, it was harder than it should've been to do that," Nilda said. "First of all, we were both still trying not to hurt her. But then it became clear that she was stronger than us."

"Separately or together?" I asked.

They traded a glance. "Almost together," Nilda said. "But we managed to hold her, the two of us, until she finally stopped struggling."

"Then I tried looking at her," Kara said.

She didn't say so, but I knew what she meant. She meant she had looked at Esja with her magical sight. Kara hadn't shown any signs of being a potential volva when she was young, or else my grandmother would've already been training her. But in the past few months, she had shown an innate talent, and both my grandmother and I had been working with her to develop it.

She didn't have the control I had, but she had a far stronger intuition than I did. I used my art skills to make up for my lack of ability to sense things the way Kara did. I might still be more powerful than she was, but her instincts were not to be ignored.

"What did you see?" I asked.

"I just wanted to see if there were signs of magic around her. Like she was under someone's spell or something," Kara said. I don't know if she knew it, but she was rubbing at her forehead again. And I guessed I knew when her headache had started.

And it must've been a doozy of a headache to keep her down the entire day. Down, and with the need to keep a bucket close at hand.

"And?" I asked.

But Kara just shook her head.

"You can't tell me about it?" I asked. Some spells were like that.

But she was shaking her head again. "No, I didn't really get to see anything. The instant I tried to open up my magical eyes to her, it was like my skull was splitting in two. White hot pain. I couldn't see. I couldn't hear. Every touch was agony."

"I'm sorry," Nilda said. I guessed she had been the one trying to touch her sister.

"You didn't know," Kara said, waving away Nilda's apology.

"I got off of Esja to try to help Kara," Nilda said. "Esja took off while I was distracted. And we haven't seen her since."

My heart sank at those words. Even if she were still in the village, it would likely take the entire evening and halfway through the night to find her.

And if she had left the village entirely? I didn't know where we'd even start to hunt for her. But the urgency in finding her straight away would be exponentially higher.

She would be in so much more danger outside of the village.

But before I could articulate any of that, Kara gave me a wry attempt at a smile. "But we're pretty sure we know where she is," she said.

CHAPTER EIGHT

ᚺ

IF KARA HAD TOLD me first that Esja had gone to the last place I would expect to her, and I had given the matter a great deal of thought before hazarding a guess, I still don't think the answer I would've come up with would be Aldís's mead hall.

And yet, that was where the three of us had gone, where Kara and Nilda both were certain we would find Esja. Because they had pulled her out of there twice before, bringing her home at a point so late in the night it was better called morning.

This mead hall was not remotely Scandinavian modern. No, being built half into a hillside, with the other half roofed with sod that sprouted with grass and wild flowers both, it was a style of architecture thoroughly from the Viking Age.

It had no windows, not even in the A-framed structure that wasn't encased in the hillside. There was only a single door, a wooden frame set in the wall whose stones showed the carbon-dark stains of generations of smoke billowing out from wood fires within.

It was the second oldest building in Villmark, I knew. Only the council hall was older. Well, that and the original home to the settlers, the caves behind the waterfall. But that wasn't so much a building as an exploited natural shelter.

"Shall we?" Nilda asked, rolling her shoulders back as if she wanted to be stretched out and ready for any possible fight.

I didn't dare ask her if it was Esja or the usual customers of this particular mead hall that she was expecting violence from.

I was too afraid the answer would be "both."

"She comes here often?" I asked, trying and failing for a jocular tone.

"Every chance she gets," Kara said with a sigh.

In truth, I didn't know how Loke would feel about his sister frequenting this place. Would he be as annoyed as the Mikkelsens? As namelessly worried as I was? Because I didn't know specifically what I was afraid she was up to, or what I was afraid would happen. I was just afraid.

But, Loke being Loke, there was always the possibility that he'd find the whole thing a huge joke. Both his sister's behavior and its effects on everyone around her.

But I didn't think it was a strong possibility.

I took the lead, pulling open the heavy oak door and stepping inside the gloomy space. We had left the last of the streetlights behind at the edge of town. They were still visible from the side of Aldís's mead hall, but where I was standing now, the hill obscured them. So at least I didn't have to wait for my eyes to adjust to the dim interior.

Even so, smells assaulted me before my eyes could pick out any details. Despite calling it a mead hall, what Aldís's was known for was a dark, bitter beer. But even that smell was only an undertone, as opening the door always changed the flow of air inside the space, sending the smells of meat grilling on the open fire pit in the center of the room racing through the doorway to permeate the night air beyond.

The smell of meat, but also a cloud of thick smoke.

And music. That was new. No one was singing, but someone was beating a slow rhythm on a drum, and someone else was accompanying on some sort of stringed instrument. Not a guitar, but something like that.

Nilda and Kara stepped into the mead hall behind me, and one of them pulled the door shut again. And instantly I was too warm. Even in the wintertime, the interior of this mead hall was stuffy and close. But now, at the end of a warmish August day, it was nearly intolerable to be trapped in a windowless place that felt like it was more fire pit than dining area.

At least it wasn't hard to find Esja. She was right there, on the far side of the fire, where the flames were brightest.

And she looked the bloom of health. Quite a contrast to the two Mikkelsen sisters, who usually looked like particularly strapping young valkyries. And quite a contrast to her usual pale picture of chronic ill health.

Her face was fuller, for one. Her cheeks rosier, although perhaps that was just because she was standing so close to the fire.

Or, rather, not standing. She was dancing. A slow, hip-circling dance. Snaky. Sensuous.

And she was dressed for it. Her white blouse looked like she'd torn the sleeves away herself, the tear leaving a fringed edge around a too-large arm hole. And she had twisted up the bottom of the blouse, forgoing any of the buttons for a mere tight knot just under her breasts.

Her white skirt was long, but it clung to her thighs in a way that left none of the curves beneath it to the imagination. And it was low-waisted, resting below the points of her hipbones, far below the level of her navel.

I hadn't even realized Esja *had* hips. But she did. She had all the curves. And she knew how to use them.

And when had her skin acquired that golden tone? After a lifetime of porcelain paleness, how had she jumped past vicious sunburn to this?

Okay, I might have been a little bit jealous about that. As a redhead, sunburns were always how five minutes in the sun ended for me if I didn't take all the precautions.

But still. I found myself turning away from Esja's snaky dance to stare dumbfounded at Nilda and Kara.

"This is new," Nilda said. She almost sounded amused. But not quite.

"Which part?" I asked.

"She's been… filling out and gaining a healthier color for a while now," Kara said. "But the outfit and the dance? That's new."

"Right," I said, turning back to Esja.

Who still hadn't noticed us enter.

No, all her attention was on the two men watching her dance. Well, truth be told, every man inside the mead hall was at least glancing her way a lot, attention torn between her display and whatever truly dire matter they were discussing with their table companions.

But two men in particular were sitting on low three-legged stools before her. They each had a tankard of beer in their hands but didn't seem to even notice, let alone partake of the contents.

The one on the left kept his blond hair cut close to his scalp, perhaps to disguise how much it was thinning on the top. I could just make out the dark blue of his eyes when Esja's movements allowed a bit more of the firelight behind her to reach him.

The one of the left was perhaps a little younger, but not much. His blond hair was darker but fuller, falling in waves just past his earlobes.

They were both built like warriors, with corded muscles on display in their sleeveless tunics and tight-fitting trousers. There was nothing modern about their clothing, not even their boots. But then there wouldn't be.

I knew the two of them well. They were part of a group of Vill-markers who thoroughly eschewed any influence from the outside world. Preferring to live as their ancestors had, or at least in the manner they ascribed to their ancestors.

"Raggi and Skefill," I said.

"Yes, that's not new," Nilda said. "Kara and I discussed it, but as much as the two of us and presumably you as well don't especially like the isolationists in general, and these two in particular, we have to admit they've never been guilty of anything."

"Yet," I said. But only because I couldn't bring myself to admit she was right. They were definitely not my favorite people to talk to in any context. But so far, they'd never broken any law or done anything to harm anyone. In fact, they were among the number who stepped up again and again to help out when the Thors were too few to cover everything that needed patrolling.

They were still working that assignment, patrolling the environs nearer to Villmark while the Thors themselves ranged further out into the wilds. And I even guessed they'd just come back from one such patrol, to judge from the mud spattering their boots. They had earned an evening of beer and society, surely.

Just not whatever society Esja was offering them now. Some other society.

Then the unseen drummer picked up the speed of the rhythm. The stringed instrument player kept up with him handily. Esja did too, at least at first. Then her feet tangled together, and she spilled over into Skefill's lap, her dirty bare feet flying high into the air.

Raggi got an eyeful before gravity brought her skirt back down again. But I had certainly seen enough of the entire situation.

I gripped the strap of my art bag and marched forward. Esja didn't notice my approach, busy as she was whispering something in Skefill's ear. But Raggi saw me, greeting me with a sour twist of his mouth.

Then Skefill saw me too, and all but shoved Esja off his lap, setting her on her feet, then belatedly realizing that his hands on her hips were perhaps too familiar as well and pulling them away from her as if her skin were liquid fire.

"Play another tune!" Esja called across the room with a decided pout on her face.

Then she finally saw me standing there. She froze like a woodland creature, half convinced that if she didn't move, I wouldn't know she was even there.

"Esja," I said, spoiling her illusion.

"They brought you here," Esja said, looking past me at Nilda and Kara. She glared at them crossly.

"They were worried about you," I said.

"But I'm perfectly fine," Esja said. She stamped the stone floor with one bare foot. As if that childish gesture could possibly sell her point.

"We need to talk, and I'd rather not do it here," I said.

Because I really hoped it wasn't going to be necessary to drag her out of here as the Mikkelsens had done before. Or worse, to have to wrestle her to the ground first.

"Of course," Esja said with a bright smile. She spun away from me in a swirl of diaphanous white skirt, but she was only bending to retrieve her shoes from a spot between the two men's stools.

"You don't have to go with her if you don't want to," Raggi said in a whisper that I was clearly meant to hear.

"It's all right. I want to. I haven't seen Ingrid in ages," Esja said.

She sounded so eager, so much like her old self. Like the two of us were about to sit down to paint in watercolors together.

But then she leaned in to press a lingering kiss to the corner of Raggi's mouth.

I was willing to bet only my presence, glowering over the two of them, kept him from leaning and taking full advantage of the moment.

Well, me, plus the two scowling valkyries I'd brought in with me. Not that they'd donned their armor or brought their weapons with them.

But, you know, not that they needed to.

Then Esja was by my side, clutching her shoes to her chest like a schoolgirl hugging her books.

Although her outfit was definitely not working with that image.

The music started up again as we headed back outside, but once the heavy door was closed behind us, the sound was muffled almost as much as the light. Now we were in the world of a Minnesotan August after dark. Heat still lingering in the tolerably humid air, insects and frogs singing their nighttime songs.

"You're going to make me go back with them, aren't you?" Esja asked as she slipped on first one shoe, then the other. Then she untied the tails of her shirt, shaking it out, then buttoning it up in the more normal manner of wearing such a shirt.

She left a lot of buttons at the top undone, but it was still an improvement.

"You don't have to stay with us if you don't want to," Nilda told her. "If you'd rather stay with Sigvin, we'll walk you to her house."

"Sigvin won't go out with me either. Not to Aldís's hall, anyway. She'll only go to Ullr's place, but everyone is so stodgy there," Esja said. She started to pout again, then seemed to remember who she was with and rethought that mannerism. It wasn't going to work with any of us the way it worked for her with the men in Aldís's hall.

"We're not going to Sigvin's either," I told her. To Nilda's and Kara's apparent surprise. "At least, not right away."

"Where are we going?" Esja asked. Then, more eagerly, "Your place?"

"Perhaps that will end up being the plan, but for now, we're going to another mead hall," I said.

For an instant, Esja looked like this was the best news ever.

Then my true meaning clicked in her mind.

"You're taking me to your grandmother?" she all but wailed.

"Yes, indeed," I said, taking her by the elbow. "We're going to that mead hall, so she can take a look at you."

"But I'm perfectly fine," Esja insisted.

And yet, she didn't try to wrest her arm out of my grasp.

Perhaps some part of her was worried about what was happening to her, too. Perhaps she was hoping my grandmother could help her with whatever was going on.

Or perhaps something else was going on, something more insidious.

Something feminine, and dark.

I leaned back to trade a look with Kara, who was trailing behind as Nilda and I flanked Esja.

Kara met my gaze. And from the grave expression on her face, she was already on alert.

But the slight nod she gave me was strangely heartening. I didn't know what was happening with Esja yet. Was she possessed? Or worse?

But the details could wait. For now, it was enough that Kara and I together had this.

And there was almost nothing my grandmother couldn't handle.

CHAPTER NINE

ᚺ

THE LIGHTS from my grandmother's mead hall were visible from the meadow, even though we headed straight towards the cave entrance and didn't walk out to the edge of the ridge to look down. It just brought a bright glow to the sky above it, like a casino if casino lights were all warm tones.

Of course, Kara and I could discern more than mere light when we looked that way. The magic that kept the mead hall protected from the notice of the world at large was no longer a pillar of power that stabbed up into the sky, but it was a constant, steady glow, even though the building itself was not in sight.

Valki was alone in the cavern by the ancestral fire, but he was lost in his own thoughts, staring into the flames. He got up with a murmured hello and a hug for his daughter-in-law, but quickly returned to his stool and his staring without so much as asking where we were off to.

Not that he needed to, really. There was only one place we could be heading.

It wasn't until we had passed the narrow cave with its massive boulder standing off to one side but always ready to be rolled over to seal the only entrance to Villmark and were crossing the sandy-floored cavern behind the waterfall itself that I remembered that Esja had never been outside of Villmark before.

She had come to a complete stop in the middle of the cavern, hugging herself as she watched the moonlight dancing through the thinnest points of that cascading water.

"My brother described this to me, but I never imagined it was so beautiful," she said. "I wished I'd brought my paints. Of course, it's too dark to paint in here."

"We can come back in daylight," I promised her. "It's even more lovely by sunlight."

"Can we?" she asked, again sounding like her old self. Always eager to paint, always eager to spend time in my company.

I felt bad for neglecting her. But I had been legitimately busy, tending to my responsibilities. Even, technically, when I'd been at my cabin. Although I'd also been waiting for Thorbjorn.

Nilda still had Esja's arm, not so much to restrain her now as to help her down the steep path that wound its way through the rocks of the bluff to the flat meadow below. The river could be heard gurgling through its shallows, but was quite out of sight beyond the tall grass and reeds from the path we were following.

Then the sounds of people talking and laughing grew louder than the sounds from the river, and the light up ahead grew stronger. We were approaching the back patio, a place on the Villmark side of the building that was mead hall by night but perfectly ordinary small town municipal building by day.

The juxtaposition was always a little jarring, walking up to a proper Viking longhouse built from heavy timbers and roofed with wooden shingles and thatch and seeing a patio of poured concrete with metal and plastic picnic tables gathered on it. The fire pit nearby was surrounded by wooden benches that could fit in with either world.

The mixed crowd that was gathered in the night air was harder to place. Some were dressed in typical Runde clothes, jeans and T-shirts with work boots or sneakers. Others wore typical Villmarker clothes, which weren't exactly like Runde clothes or like the rustic outfits

Raggi, Skefill and the others in Aldís's mead hall had been wearing. The cut was reminiscent of the Viking era, certainly, but the materials were usually modern, both the type of fabric and the patterns and colors they sported. And the seams were all machine made.

But all those people were standing together, drinking or playing card games, without anyone seeming to notice what anyone around them looked like.

That was all part of my grandmother's magic. The Villmarkers knew where they were and who they were carousing with. But the people of Runde would leave at the end of the night only remembering that they had been hanging with old friends.

If they ever wondered why they never seemed to run into any of those friends anywhere but the mead hall, it was only a passing thought, gone in a moment.

We slipped through the crowd on the patio and headed into the mead hall itself through the back door. The interior was about as different from Aldís's mead hall as it was possible to get, considering they both shared a basic architectural aesthetic.

There were no windows, that was true. But the ceiling here was high overhead, and the smoke from the fire pits rose up past the timber frame beams to disappear. Not that there were any chimneys up there. My grandmother wouldn't risk anyone wondering where all the smoke was coming from.

But it didn't linger inside her hall, either. Just a touch of magic, and it was all whisked away.

The timber frame beams and pillars that held them up were all carved with Nordic designs, the honey-gold of their polished surfaces reflecting the light from the fire and the lamps to fill the space with cheery light.

One end of the room was all fireplace, but its roaring flames were only for light. A different sort of spell kept the heat from the fire at a level that gently warmed the entire space, no matter how far from the fireplace it was. And it never got too hot or too stifling.

I looked around at the people gathered at the long tables, drinking tankards of beer or ale or glasses of my grandmother's mead, but while I recognized faces here and there, none of them were my close friends. There was no sign of Andrew or Jessica, or my other friend Michelle or her new boyfriend, Nate.

Which was just as well. I wasn't sure what my grandmother would find when she looked at Esja, but I was sure that free time wasn't going to be on my schedule anywhere in the near future.

My grandmother watched us approach where she stood behind her bar, dispensing glasses of mead. She took one look at Esja between Nilda and me, then wiped her hands on a towel before heading to the door down to the cellar without a word.

We followed.

The stairway was dark, and even though I knew I wasn't anywhere near tall enough to have to worry, I still stooped as I walked. I knew there were heavy timbers holding up the floor above us, and in the dark they always felt closer to my head than they were.

My grandmother lit a lamp once she had reached the room at the bottom of the stairs. Then she turned to look at Esja more closely.

"Kara got a headache when she tried to examine Esja for signs of magic," I warned her.

"Headache?" my grandmother repeated, giving Kara a measuring look.

"Sudden and intense pain. Couldn't see. Couldn't hear," Kara said tersely.

"Couldn't bear to be touched," Nilda added, still flushing guiltily at the memory. "She vomited five times."

"Interesting," my grandmother said, turning her attention back to Esja.

"I feel perfectly fine," Esja said. But she was all but whispering now.

Maybe that was just because she was talking to my mormor now, and my mormor intimidated everyone. No one would enjoy being on the receiving end of the intense study she was subjecting Esja to just now.

But I was starting to see what Nilda and Kara had meant about her moodiness. Esja's entire behavior kept changing, suddenly and without warning. So far, it had all seemed perfectly logical. She had been caught in a moment she'd rather I hadn't seen. But she always enjoyed being the center of my attention. And yet, not so much the center of my grandmother's attention. All mood shifts that made sense.

But it also felt kind of wrong.

"You had reason to examine her for spells," my grandmother said. It wasn't quite a question.

"Esja has been behaving oddly. Out of character," Kara said. "This morning she was particularly combative."

"I said I was sorry for that," Esja said. "I didn't get much sleep last night."

"Because you were out carousing until dawn," Nilda said.

"I was with friends," Esja said. "Do you know what that's like? To have friends? To be able to spend time with them? Of course you do. You always have. Is it really so strange that I want to do such things, now that I finally can?"

"Making up for lost time?" my grandmother asked her.

"Exactly," Esja said.

"Your brother kept you home," my grandmother said. Then she looked Esja right in the eye, so intensely even I flinched a little. And she was *my* grandmother. "Against your will?"

"No," Esja said, twisting her hands together. "Not exactly. I mean, I was sick. For a long time. But I feel better now."

"Do you?" Again, that tone in my grandmother's voice. Like answering her questions was just falling in to some sort of trap she was laying.

"Don't I look better?" Esja asked. She sounded desperately eager to please, but then she stopped twisting her hands together and lifted her chin.

"Yes. You do," my grandmother said. "You are the very bloom of good health. Doesn't that worry you?"

"I should be worried that I feel well?" Esja asked.

"I would be worried if my lifelong illness just suddenly went away," my grandmother said.

"No one ever found its cause. Not even you," Esja said. Not quite a challenge in her tone, but very close to one. But then she went on in her usual meeker tone. "No one knew the cause, so I don't think it's strange that the cure is equally mysterious."

"Maybe something in the house was making her sick?" I said. "The house *is* in very rough shape."

"This is true," my grandmother allowed. Then she looked at Kara.

"Her personality changes have been extreme," she said.

"Which is worrying, but not necessarily the result of a magical influence," my grandmother said. "She's been through some pretty big life changes. And she's at an age where lots of young people discover who they really are."

"She's been so… well, extreme," Nilda said, borrowing her sister's word.

"Yes, and I admitted that was worrying," my grandmother said. "But come, the three of us will take a look at her. If there's something there, we can work together to resolve it, I'm sure. But if not? Then I suggest you attempt talking with Signi one more time."

"You knew I was there before?" Esja asked, as surprised as I or Nilda or Kara.

My grandmother just smiled her most enigmatic smile.

"What did Signi tell you?" I asked.

But my grandmother just directed that smile at me. "I know she's not practicing in her modern world sense, but there is still doctor/patient confidentiality, surely."

"But she *did* tell you?" I pressed.

"I know what I need to know," my grandmother said.

She was still smiling, but Esja was really squirming now. Like she could guess what Signi had told my grandmother. And she knew it wasn't good.

"What do we need to do?" Kara asked. She was clearly nervous to try this again. I wasn't eager to experience headaches and vomiting myself.

But my grandmother just held out a hand to each of us. "If we channel the power together, I'm sure we'll all be fine. We are in my mead hall, after all. The protective magics here make this the best place to try something potentially risky. Which I'm not even sure this is."

"Really?" I asked, taking her hand, then holding out my other to Kara. Who was hesitating.

"Kara, dear, your intuition is strong," my grandmother said. "Stronger than Ingrid's. Maybe even stronger than mine. But your magic is still unpracticed. You didn't shield yourself well enough. Granted, that's because I haven't taught you how, yet. But we're safe now."

Kara bit at her lip, but then in a rush slipped one hand into mine and took my grandmother's with the other.

Esja was now trapped between the interlocked hands of the three of us. She was twisting her hands again, but she wasn't trying to get away. She just looked nervous, like she was afraid of whatever diagnosis we were about to make.

There was no headache, sudden or otherwise. There was no vomiting. There was just the gentle flow of magic through our joined hands, magic that wove its way in and out of the foundational walls of the mead hall cellar around us.

I saw power glowing from Kara on my right, and even more power glowing from my grandmother on my left.

But Esja looked no more magical than Nilda, who was waiting at the bottom of the stairs. There was a small light, because every living thing has some magic in it.

But there was no pattern to it like a spell. And no great power to it like something malevolent was possessing Esja.

She just looked like what she was, a confused young woman not dealing well with a sudden overabundance of liberty.

My grandmother dropped my hand and Kara's at the same time. Then she pulled Esja's stiff body into a tight hug.

"Promise me three things," she said to Esja.

"Yes, anything," Esja said.

"When you long for company, for—as Nilda would say—carousing, I ask that you come here where I know you will be safe."

"I will," Esja said.

I don't know if she meant it. I couldn't read her tone well enough to measure honesty or sincerity.

But when I saw a blossom of light briefly illuminate her forehead, I knew it didn't matter what she had meant. She was bound by her word to my grandmother, whether she liked it or not.

"I want you to continue seeing Signi, just to talk with her. About whatever you like, and she won't tell me any of it unless she knows that I, as a volva, need to know. Short of that, your secrets are your own. Understood?"

"Yes. I will," Esja said. A second light blossomed on her forehead and then was gone.

"And the third thing?" I asked.

"Your brother is coming back to you," my grandmother said to Esja. "Believe that. Don't doubt that. Ever. That's the third promise I need from you."

Esja's chin started to tremble, and tears welled in the corners of her eyes. But she just wiped them away with the back of her hand, clenched her jaw until the trembling stopped, and said, "I will. I promise."

The third light flashed, then died away.

"I'm sure you're tired, dear," my grandmother said. "Why don't you go home with Nilda and Kara? Ingrid and I will call on you soon, but in the meantime, remember your promises."

"I will, volva," Esja said. She sounded stronger now.

Then she spun on her heel and all but ran back up the stairs to the mead hall above.

"Are we sure there's nothing magical wrong with her?" I asked, because I had to.

"As much as anyone could be sure of such things," my grandmother said.

Which really wasn't much of a comfort at all.

But then she added, "Helping Esja get to a better place inside her own mind is the best plan. Because you are right to be worried, both of you. There are things that would try to use her, to get at us but mainly to get at Loke. A stronger, more confident Esja with a bit of magical knowledge is going to be a much tougher target."

"We can't just lock her down ourselves?" Kara asked.

The look my grandmother pinned on her was frightening in a way that brought that sudden hailstorm back to mind.

"She has been locked down by outside forces quite enough, as I'm sure you would agree," she said. I could see Kara steeling her spine, fighting the temptation to cringe away from my grandmother's sudden anger.

"Couldn't we teach her to shield herself first and then help her emotionally?" I asked. Kara shot me a quick, grateful look when my grandmother's attention swept off her to me.

But my grandmother's anger was gone as quickly as it came. "I'm afraid that wouldn't be wise. She needs to be stronger before giving her any magical knowledge at all would be anything other than a tragic mistake. Trust me on this."

"We should probably catch up with her," Nilda said, already edging her way up the stairs.

"Yes, get her home and get her some sleep," my grandmother said. "We can discuss this further later."

I gave her a quick hug goodbye, then followed the sisters up the stairs.

I hadn't seen any sign of magic around Esja. Neither from her nor affecting her.

But something still felt wrong with her.

I hoped my grandmother was right. I hoped that talking with Signi would help Esja get a handle on things.

But I needed to come up with a plan. Just in case what I felt but couldn't see turned out to be a problem.

Yeah, it was going to be a little tricky to plan for the complete unknown. But I had to do *something*.

CHAPTER TEN

ᚺ

THE AIR WAS JUST humid enough to help the heat linger into the night without being stifling, and the walk back up to Villmark was actually pleasant. The stars overhead were so bright it felt like they were hanging lower in the sky, the Milky Way a visible streak across it all.

The cleanup from the storm was well in the past now, and the cobblestone roads were neatly swept. There was an occasional breeze rustling through the branches of the trees and shrubberies hidden away in the walled front gardens of the homes we passed. The whispering of the leaves was never loud enough to drown out the chorus from the insects and amphibians, but did encourage the blossoming plants to release their scents into the air.

It was too nice of a walk to interrupt it with discussion of darker things. I think we were all of a mind on that score.

So none of us said a word until we were back in the Mikkelsens' house on the west side of the village. We all passed through to the living room and sat down on the sofa and chairs.

But I could tell that Esja was getting anxious. She was fidgeting more, and looking back towards the corridor that led to the front door. As if that way lay freedom.

"Nilda, Kara, could I have a moment alone with Esja?" I asked.

"Of course," Nilda said. "We're on duty at the fire tonight, anyway. You're okay here if we head out?"

"We'll be fine," I assured her with a smile.

She and Kara traded a look that said my words weren't received with the amount of comfort I had intended them. And I understood that. Whatever had happened with Esja that morning, I had yet to see signs of the same behavior myself. And they knew I hadn't. So they thought I was underestimating what it had been, or maybe even disbelieving their account. But in the end she just nodded, and the two of them headed upstairs to change before going out.

Esja perched on the very edge of the chair Nilda had been sitting in that morning. I wondered if she had chosen it because she wanted to sit with her back to the door that was calling to her.

Or because she wanted to sit with her back to the damage on the wall that she had caused.

I sat down on the sofa and tried to collect my thoughts. I was weary, but I knew that sleep was going to be elusive that night. Even if I managed to depart this house feeling like I had left things in a reasonable condition of order.

Which I didn't think was likely.

Esja was fidgeting again, twisting her hands together. She looked like she was about to speak. But I didn't want to give her the opportunity to beg off. I had to speak first.

"You know you're bound by the promises you made to my grandmother," I said to her.

"Yes, that was clear," Esja said. "I will only go to her mead hall, I will talk with Signi about things, and I will make myself believe that my brother is coming back to me."

"Did you doubt that?" I asked.

"Don't you?" she countered. But not aggressively. No, the hesitant look she shot my way through her eyelashes was downright shy.

"I *want* to believe he's okay," I admitted.

"You don't know what's going on with him any better than I do," she said. Not a question.

"I'm afraid not," I said. "I know he is still with Thorbjorn. My cat

Mjolner checks in with them every day or so. If anything had changed, Mjolner would find a way to tell me. And if they needed me, I would know."

"That helps," she said, and her hands stopped twisting.

I thought about what I had seen when I had drawn her house, but I didn't want to ask her about it directly. Instead, I asked, "When do you think you started to feel differently? Was it right after your brother left?"

"That's just the thing, I don't feel different," she said. She was looking at her hands, now still in her lap, and not at me. And she barely spoke above a whisper.

"That felt like you, dancing in the mead hall earlier?" I asked as delicately as I could.

"Yes," she said. Her cheeks flushed with color, but she still didn't look up at me. "I like music as much as I like painting. I just never had an opportunity to experience it much before."

"Mormor has all kinds of music at her mead hall," I told her. "A lot of it is very good for dancing."

"I look forward to trying it out," she said. But her tone was very neutral.

"Why did you end up at Aldís's mead hall?" I asked her.

"It's the closest," she said with a shrug.

I summoned a mental map of Villmark and quickly realized this was true. Certainly, my grandmother's mead hall was not only the farthest, but also on the other side of the waterfall. She might have thought she couldn't go down there without an escort or an invitation or something. Or it had never occurred to her that it was an option at all.

She really had lived a very closed-up life. And she deserved a lifetime of many more experiences than she'd had so far.

But trying to experience it all at once was going to flame her out.

"Your behavior was a little extreme," I told her. "I suppose you just didn't know how others would see you. What sort of attention you were drawing. But it would be better for you to be with company. Friends."

"Nilda and Kara are always so busy with their duties," Esja said. Even as we heard the front door quietly closing behind the sisters as they headed back out into the night.

"There's always Sigvin," I said.

Esja opened her mouth like she was about to say something, then scoffed out a little laugh before closing it again.

"What?" I asked, genuinely curious.

"Sigvin likes my brother a lot," she said, one corner of her mouth angling up in a wry grin.

"I've noticed," I said.

"When she drinks, it comes up. A lot," Esja said.

"Okay, I could see how that would be annoying for you," I said.

"You could go out with me?" she said, finally looking up at me, but in the shy through-her-lashes way again.

"I don't go out much," I admitted.

"But you *could*," she pressed. "I mean, you're kind of all alone, just like I am. When Thorbjorn is away. Like he is now."

"Like Nilda and Kara, I have a lot of duties," I said.

"And I have nothing at all," she said, looking down at the hands on her lap again. But this time as if she were angry at them for being so empty.

"We can find a way for you to contribute," I said. "We've been letting you guide us as to how active you felt like being, and at the very least, I think we can all agree that you're ready to be more active."

Which was a really oblique way of putting it.

But it brought that grin back to her face. It wasn't as wide as her brother's, really more just a crooked lift to one side.

But it felt like their grins came from the same place. It was downright eerie, actually.

"I feel perfectly healthy," she said. "I don't know why. But I haven't had a bad day since the first week I came to the village. Not a one."

"That's good to hear," I said.

But then I had to bring the conversation around to what I really wanted to know.

"Do you think it's because of the house?" I asked.

"Do you?" she countered. This time, her glance up at me was challenging.

"It's a possibility," I said. "Have you been back there since your brother left?"

"Twice," she said without needing even a moment's thought. "Once during the first week I was at Sigvin's house. I had to get some things I had forgotten when I'd packed the first time."

"Was that before or after you stopped feeling sick?" I interrupted to ask her.

She looked surprised by the question. Then she looked up towards the ceiling as she consulted her memory. "Before. I went to the house and then back to Sigvin's all right, but the next morning it was like I was completely exhausted. I didn't get out of bed for two days."

"And the second time?"

"I didn't get sick the second time," she said, again without having to think about it.

"And when was that?" I asked.

"Just last week," she said with a shrug.

"You needed something else?" I asked. If so, I knew what I had to say next. I was prepared to offer to fetch anything else she needed, to keep her from needing to do it herself.

But she was already shaking her head. "No, I just wanted to see. I felt stronger. More than that, I felt like I was more in the world than I'd ever been in my life. Like smells are stronger, colors are brighter, everything is just *more*. Like all my life, I was a ghost, but now I'm finally becoming a real living person."

"And you wanted to test if the house would change you back to a ghost?" I asked. I tried not to sound as horrified as I felt at the thought. She really needed to talk to me about these things before she just tried them.

But, again, she was already shaking her head. "No, I didn't think it could hurt me anymore. Not now. No, if I thought it could, I'd never have gone back."

"Then why?" I asked, at a complete loss.

"I wanted to see what it looked like," she said. "My memories of it were fading, like it had been as much a ghost as I was, but while I was getting stronger, it was going away. I wanted to see it and smell it and *feel* it before it was gone entirely." Then she scoffed out a self-deprecating laugh. "I know that sounds crazy."

"No, it really doesn't," I said. "I just wish you'd told me, or at least Nilda and Kara, about all this sooner."

"I don't want to be any trouble," she said.

I just stopped myself from glancing up at the hole in the wall behind her. She sounded sincere. She sounded like her old self.

But I hadn't been there when she had been throwing things. I had to keep that in mind.

"So you walked down to your house and went inside and explored it, then came back here, and nothing happened?" I asked.

"I wouldn't say nothing happened," she admitted, twisting a lock of hair behind her ear.

"Did you see something inside the house?" I asked. My fingers itched to pull my sketchbook out, to search my drawings from that afternoon for clues.

But she was laughing. It was her usual gentle, soft laugh. But it set every hair on the back of my neck on end.

"No, outside the house," she said.

"The hailstorm," I guessed.

"Yes, the hailstorm," she said. "I was about to walk back to town when I saw the clouds rolling in. So I ran back inside and stood in the doorway and watched all that hail come pounding down. I've never seen anything like that before. It was..."

"Scary," I finished for her.

But she shook her head. "No, exhilarating. I wanted so badly to run out and dance in it! But I had to wait until it was just rain. Like I said, I'm not crazy."

No, I didn't think she was crazy.

But there was definitely something going on with her. Some sort of change.

I wanted to tell myself it was a good thing. She was so much healthier than I had ever seen her. Stronger. And happier, despite her acting out.

But I couldn't set that acting out aside either. I hoped my grandmother was right, and this was just normal young adult stuff. I knew a few classmates from my high school days who had... shall we call them very *eventful* freshmen years at college?

Working full time while going to art school full time hadn't left that sort of party lifestyle an option for me. But I knew it was pretty far from rare. And all those classmates had come through it in the end, straightened out and took their lives more seriously before things got too bad for them.

Maybe Esja would too. Although I didn't relish the thought of watching her stumble down that path. It had been hard enough for friends I didn't care so much about as I cared about Esja.

But what if something more was going on with her?

Had the hailstorm done something to her?

Or worse, had she summoned the hailstorm in the first place? Unknowingly?

Or knowingly?

I half-closed my eyes and looked at her again, studying the patterns of magic around her. She looked like a perfectly ordinary young woman, glowing a little brighter in Villmark than she had down in Runde, but that was just the effect of crossing the barrier. It left lingering spell residue like fairy dust on everyone who passed through it.

I saw no hint of dark feminine power in or around her. She was just herself.

So why didn't I trust what I was seeing with my own eyes? Why was my gut still screaming "danger?"

CHAPTER ELEVEN

Esja went meekly up to bed after our little interview, and I stretched out on the sofa.

For all of thirty seconds. Then I was sitting up again.

Just as I suspected, sleep was going to be elusive. Until I knew what was going on, there was no way I was going to get my mind to stop trying to work the problem.

So I dug out my sketchbook and looked over all my drawings from the storm, but especially the ones I had drawn that afternoon at Esja and Loke's house.

It had been the heart of the storm, I was sure of that.

But that was all I was sure of.

I turned to a fresh page, dug my charcoal pencils out of my bag, and sat back cross-legged on the couch to draw.

Usually, when I do this sort of magical drawing, I go into a fugue state. I'm scarcely aware of what I'm doing while I'm doing it. My own drawings are a wonder and a mystery to me when I look at them afterwards. Almost as if someone else had drawn them, although they are always clearly in my style.

This wasn't that.

No, this time, I was aware as I drew. It felt like I was directing things in a way that I didn't usually feel when trying to use my magic.

Maybe I was growing as a volva.

I remembered a similar moment in my early teens when my focus on drawing had shifted from detail after detail to just... drawing.

Not that I couldn't still get hung up in details. But I didn't need to focus my mind that way to make a drawing. I didn't have to think of what I was trying to do, and the best techniques to accomplish those things. I could just draw, and the skills would be there.

Maybe this was like that.

But whatever the reason, I found myself drawing the shore of a lake with a storm far out over the waters, threatening and dark.

The waves of the lake had a lot of menace in them too, when my pencil passed over them again and again. Those were sharp-edged waves, hungry to devour ships.

Of course there was nothing in the drawing to indicate it, but I knew it was deep, that lake. Not bottomless, but crushingly deep. I felt the depth of it as my charcoal skittered over the page.

I expected the storm to start raining down Hagall runes, but it didn't. Instead, it seemed to turn around and around about itself. Each pass made the whole thing darker. And it was funneling down.

Not a sea spout, or rather a lake spout. No, and it wasn't like a tornado either.

I just kept drawing it, waiting for the details my hand innately knew how to render to summon some meaning in my thinking brain.

And then some jagged vertical details started to make sense. It wasn't a weather phenomenon at all, what I was drawing.

It was the trunk of a tree. An immense tree, one that extended far above the reach of the storm clouds that dominated the top of the page. And far below the surface of the water. Maybe even further down than the bottom of that lake. I wasn't sure.

I had drawn the World Tree on many occasions. Viking imagery had always called to me even as a kid who didn't know her own heritage, and most of the portfolio from art school that I hoped would land me book illustration jobs were depictions of scenes from Norse myths.

I was no stranger to the tree Yggdrasil.

And yet I had never drawn it like this. So immense.

So menacing.

Then the charcoal in my hand crumbled. That sometimes happens. But in that moment, it felt like a bad omen.

A very bad omen indeed.

I took out my pencils and started a new drawing. This time I deliberately drew Yggdrasil, Yggdrasil as it was as the central pillar of my cabin in the woods. The cabin's former owner had carved its likeness out of wood, every leaf and branch, every creature that inhabited its limbs. Like the eagle Vidofnir, who sat atop the highest branches of the trees, and like Nidhogg, the dragon who ate at its roots.

And Ratatosk, the squirrel who ran between the two of them, carrying the messages they sent to each other, which were all taunts and insults.

I always loved that squirrel.

I liked drawing dragons as well, but this time, I found myself sketching in three shadows behind the dragon. Three figures lurking in the darkness, watching as Nidhogg destroyed the roots of the World Tree.

I guessed they were the Norns, the Norse version of the Fates. Aside from their duty as determiners of destiny, they also repaired the damage Nidhogg did to the tree. They would pour water from Urd's well over the chewed roots of the tree to heal the damage, but that dragon would always chew through it all over again afterwards.

Such was life in the Norse myths. A constant battle just to say in the middle.

Still, as I sat back and looked at what I had drawn, I didn't think the reaches of water that stretched across the entire bottom of the page looked much like the water from a well.

It looked like the lake again. I sensed depth there, so much depth.

But I didn't know what any of this meant.

I did a few more drawings, but the results were not as good. Both artistically but also magically. They told me nothing, and my tired hand was making mistake after mistake.

I probably should've just set it aside and called it a night.

But I didn't. I kept at it.

Or, at least, I tried to.

But at some point, I did stop drawing. My head rolled back against the back of the couch and I fell deeply asleep, pencil still in hand, sketchbook still open on my cross-legged lap.

The sudden meowing close to my ear woke me with a start. And I tried to scramble to my feet.

But quickly found my legs had gone completely numb from the hips down.

Yeah, falling asleep while sitting cross-legged is a terrible idea.

I stumbled against the coffee table and managed not to fall, although the hard sitting down on the floor I did was pretty fall-adjacent.

I had a moment to realize just how numb my legs were. Under my hands, their flesh felt corpse-cold. Definitely not good.

Then the pins and needles started. With a vengeance.

I clenched my jaw to keep from crying out as the pain washed over me.

But it finally washed back out again. The pins and needles faded back to their more customary, merely uncomfortable feeling. I stretched out my legs and shook my knees up and down a little. Hoping that would hurry the process along.

Mjolner, meanwhile, hopped down from the back of the couch to perch on the coffee table before me. He sat primly with his tail around his paws, blinking at me dispassionately. Then, slowly, he raised a single paw, flicked it, then began bathing his ears.

"There was a reason for that? Or were you just worried when I didn't come home?" I asked him as I massaged first one leg than the other. It would probably be safe to try standing soon.

Probably.

Mjolner stopped bathing his ears to fix me with his yellow-green eyes.

They were distinctly accusatory.

"Sorry. I just figured you knew I was here," I said, climbing back up onto the couch. I put my sketchbook and pencils on the coffee table beside the bathing cat, then gathered up the throw pillows at one end. The blanket Kara had been using was still there, neatly folded at the other end of the couch. I shook it out, then curled up on the couch in a far more sensible position for sleeping.

Mjolner watched me until I was settled. Then he climbed over me to wedge himself between the back of my neck and the back of the couch. He turned so that his spine was curled against my neck, and then he immediately dropped off to sleep.

The sound of his whirring purr soon had me doing the same.

At least until I was woken again, this time by a hand on my shoulder shaking me hard.

"Ingrid, wake up," Kara was saying, still shaking me, although my eyes were quite open.

"Esja?" I guessed as I sat up, ignoring Mjolner's soft sound of protest. He'd have the pillows to himself now, anyway.

"She's not here," Kara said. "Her window was left open. I don't think she ever got in her bed at all."

CHAPTER TWELVE

ᚺ

IT WASN'T LIKE I didn't know where to start looking. Sure, it was closer to dawn than midnight. But still. Not even my grandmother's mead hall was closed yet. The carousing at Aldís's mead hall was probably just ramping up.

"The promise bound her, though," Kara said, not for the first time, as we jogged west on the road that led out of the village. She was wearing her fairly typical look of leggings and short-sleeved, loose-fitting summer tunic. But because she'd woken me just after coming back from the ancestral fire, she was still wearing her sword at her hip.

And, knowing Kara, she probably had at least three knives in less obvious places.

I hoped we didn't run into any trouble, but it still felt better knowing that at least one of us was prepared.

"If Esja was with my grandmother, she would've told us," I said to her. "And she wouldn't have pretended to go to bed and then sneaked out to get there in the first place."

"I'm not arguing either of those points," Kara said. "I'm just saying, we saw the spell take hold."

I stopped jogging, catching on to Kara's elbow so she would do the same. She turned to face me, not even the slightest bit out of breath, waiting for me to speak with her arms crossed. Like what I had to say had better be good.

"We saw the spell take hold of *Esja*," I told her.

"And before that, we saw that she wasn't possessed," Kara said.

"In that moment," I said.

Kara narrowed her eyes at me skeptically. "If she had ever been possessed, there would've been signs of it. Little threads of spells still clinging to her. Or, at least, that would be how it would look to me. But there wasn't any, not a single glowing fragment of a thread. No one could erase every hint of magic residue from her. Not after a spell powerful enough to take over her mind."

"No one?" I challenged.

She looked ever so slightly contrite, but then screwed her expression back to her former stern look. "I remember what Halldis did to you. When she was roaming free, she had the power to possess people. I'm not arguing against that. I'm just saying, even though I didn't know how to see magic at that point, when I saw you after, I could tell something massive had happened to you. And I'm sure your grandmother, with her honed perceptions, didn't even have to try to see the magic hanging all over you."

"Halldis wasn't trying to hide anything," I said. But then realized that wasn't entirely true. "Well, she didn't have time to try hiding what she did to me. But she did hide what she was doing to Roarr. My grandmother looked at him as well, very closely. But she could never tell how much Halldis had been controlling his actions."

"You think this is Halldis?" Kara asked.

"No," I said. "She's safely secured in her cell, deep in the lower caverns behind the waterfall. I've been in that cell, and I've seen her, what's left of her after months of captivity. She's not doing this."

"Your grandmother said she couldn't tell how much of what Roarr was doing was because Halldis was compelling him, and how much was just him choosing to go along, right?" Kara asked.

"That's what she's always told me," I said. "I'm thinking maybe it's the same thing now. Two things happening at once, I mean. Some of this is Esja's behavior, and some of this is something else. Not Halldis, but something."

"Do you know something I don't know?" she asked, narrowing her eyes.

"No," I admitted with another sigh. "If anything, I know less than you do."

"Because you keep questioning everything?" Kara said.

I shrugged. But yeah, that was what I had been thinking. My cup of knowledge was decidedly empty. Because I kept dumping out what wasn't useful.

But I needed to find what should be filling it, or it was a pointless exercise. "Someone or something taught Halldis what magic she knew, because it certainly wasn't my grandmother. And it didn't all come from that amulet. She had power of her own before Roarr gave her that amulet. But Halldis has never revealed a bit about that. Ever."

Kara fiddled with the hilt of her sword as she pondered that. As if she wished that the solution to our problem could be so easy as to simply hack away at it.

Or maybe I was projecting. *I* certainly wished it could be so easy.

"What are we going to do if even our own perceptions can't be trusted?" she asked at last.

Which was a very good question.

"For one, we can put a guard on Esja day and night," I said, gesturing for us to continue our jog to the mead hall.

"Do you mean put her in the caves?" Kara asked.

I hadn't. But now that she said it, it wasn't a bad idea. That was where Villmark put everyone who couldn't coexist with the rest of the people of the village for one reason or another.

Like Halldis, who had actively used her magic to kill and coverup her killing.

But also like Bera, who had also killed someone. Sigvin's sister, in fact. But in Bera's case, she was, as the modern world would call it, not guilty by reason of insanity. She was currently receiving all the care that Signi, Bera's own parents, and the rest of Villmark could give her. But it was never going to be enough for it to be safe for Bera to walk freely through our streets again.

Did Esja belong there?

No, I decided. Not even for her own safety, or to protect her from herself. And not just because what she longed for above all things was her newfound freedom, and locking her up would be intolerably cruel.

The fact was, she hadn't broken any of the village's laws. And running off to charm the men in mead halls wasn't even close to being an offense.

But if she was bold enough to crawl out a window the minute she got upstairs after telling me specifically that she was going to bed, she definitely needed closer watching. And less trust.

This time, we could hear the music playing as we approached the door to the mead hall. There were a couple of drummers beating out rhythms together, and a host of other stringed instruments and woodwinds playing along. And it sounded like everyone else in the hall was hooting and hollering as they clapped along.

So it wasn't entirely surprising to see Esja once more dancing in the center of the hall, spinning so close to the fire her lifted skirt was flirting with the flames.

But she was no longer dancing alone. Now she was in the arms of a man I recognized but didn't know by name. One of the farmers from south of the village, I thought. And it looked like he was getting a little handsy.

Even as Kara and I watched, Esja laughed and spun out of his reach. His fingers grasped for the trailing folds of her skirt, but they slipped out of his reach as her spin changed course.

Now she was in Raggi's arms. And if his handsiness was more than the little bit of her last dance partner... well, to be fair, Esja was the handsiest of them all.

The room around us was stifling, full of smoke and the smell of roasting meat almost cloyingly strong, but also full of the pounding of feet and the clapping of hands. And the never-ending build of the music.

Kara was trying to say something to me, but I couldn't catch more than the hint of her voice close to my ear.

I took out my bronze wand, but I had no idea what I could do with it. I'd love to blow open the door and send a stiff breeze through this hall. I was starting to smell the scents that were lurking under the prevalent meat odor. There were a lot of sweaty men here, men who worked at hard labor all day and didn't necessarily wash up before coming to the mead hall for a pint.

But having once summoned a tornado that wiped out my grandmother's beloved cabin, I was a little reluctant to try creating a wind. That had been an accident, when my powers were far newer to me, and I had done it with a different, cursed wand. But still. Lesson learned.

So I decided to try one of my grandmother's favorite techniques instead. I magically oomphed up my voice.

"Esja," I said.

And the walls around us quaked, sending a few showers of earth from the sod roof above cascading down on everyone in the mead hall. The music came to a halt with a screech of a flute or two.

I had oomphed it too much.

But I certainly had everyone's attention. The stomping and clapping had ceased. The only sounds now were the crackles and hisses from the fire pit, and the labored breathing of the now still dancers.

"Esja," I said again, but this time in my normal voice. "You are coming with me. Now."

"She's a free woman, volva," Raggi said, tightening his arms around Esja.

"This doesn't concern you, Raggi," Kara said. She was standing on my right side, but a step behind me. Still, even without seeing her, I sensed the shift in her posture as she put her hand to the hilt of her sword. She could have it drawn in a blink of an eye.

There was a rustling around the room as a few of the other patrons mimicked that motion. We were one false move away from a full-on bar fight, albeit one with swords and axes and war hammers.

"Esja is going to come with me of her own free will," I said, raising my hands placatingly. As if I had been the one making threatening moves.

But Kara followed my lead, releasing her hold on her sword and shifting to a more relaxed posture.

A deceptively relaxed posture, although I didn't think anyone in the hall was actually deceived. They all knew her well enough to know how quick and deadly she could be with that sword. And no one wanted to test her.

But her relaxing first let them all do likewise without losing face.

Only Raggi remained tense. He kept Esja tightly in his grasp, but shifted her to a position a little more behind him. As if I might try to pull her away from him by force.

"Esja," I said.

"You made a promise," Kara added.

Esja was looking at us over Raggi's shoulder, her eyes just barely visible because of their height difference. But at Kara's words, I saw those eyes flinch a little. As if just the word "promise" had triggered a sudden headache.

Indeed, she pressed her forehead to Raggi's shoulder for a moment. I almost thought she was about to swoon.

But then she lifted her head to look up at him. She whispered a few words to him, too softly for me to hear.

He didn't seem to like those words. He shook his head at her and clung to her even more tightly than before.

But she gave him a shy little smile and whispered again. Maybe the same words, maybe something different. But whatever they were, they had the desired effect.

He let her go.

She brushed past him, letting one hand linger on his forearm for as long as it was possible as she slowly made her way across the room to Kara and me.

"Do you want to explain?" Kara asked her sternly.

But before Esja could answer—if indeed she had any intention of answering—I said, "No. Not here."

Kara scowled, but nodded, motioning for Esja to precede her out the door.

I trailed behind, letting my gaze sweep the room one last time. There were a few patrons who turned their faces away, some even pulling up hoods as they pretended a sudden interest in the drinks in front of them. But that was pretty common in this particular mead hall. Every time I set foot inside, they let me know this wasn't a welcome place for meddling volvas.

But what I didn't see—what I had actually been looking for—was any hint of magic. And very little sign of anything feminine.

If there was someone or something lurking in this place who kept luring Esja here, they weren't here now. And there was no sign of any such magic lingering.

Which it would do. The most powerful version of that spell I had seen had been the one used to lure two of the Thors' cousins out into the winter night to be picked up by the Wild Hunt. And that had left such clear signs I had been able not only to stop it, but to trace it back to its source.

And I had been much less skilled then.

I went back outside to where Kara and Esja were waiting for me. Esja was still barefoot this time, but she had put her outfit back to rights while I had lingered inside the hall.

I looked her over carefully, but again I saw nothing.

"You have to look when she's really behaving oddly," Kara said to me, as if she could tell what I was doing.

Esja flushed but only said, "Can we just go home now?"

"You broke your promise," I said to her. "Do you remember that?"

"I didn't *mean* to come here," Esja said. "I just wanted to take a walk."

"You climbed out the window," I said. "If all you needed was a little fresh air, why not just use the door?"

Esja said nothing.

"I'll sleep in her room," Kara said wearily. "Then we'll try sorting this out in the morning."

"We'll both sleep in her room," I said. "After I seal that window shut."

Esja looked like she wanted to object, but she deflated again without a word, just a sullen nod. And we three walked back to Kara's house to try a second time to put an end to the endless night.

CHAPTER THIRTEEN

H

IT WAS a good thing that Kara had been there, because I would've made a terrible guard on my own. I didn't wake until nearly midday, and found myself alone on Esja's bed with Mjolner purring on the pillow just behind my neck.

I hadn't even been in the bed the night before. I had been in a chair I had moved to rest against the closed bedroom door, blocking the way out.

I don't know who moved me, or how they managed it without waking me. It was equal parts puzzling and embarrassing.

But both of those feelings paled in comparison to the surge of panic I felt when I realized that Esja wasn't there. I sat up so suddenly that Mjolner yowled in protest, throwing back the covers and preparing to bolt for the door.

Then I saw the note on the nightstand.

"You needed the sleep. Esja is downstairs with me. Kara."

Mjolner looked back over his shoulder, glaring at me with his sleepy yellow-green eyes.

"Sorry," I said to him as I set the note aside. "Go back to sleep. I'm sure there's a reason why you're so tired."

I wasn't quite being sarcastic. But he just blinked at me and meowed in a way that I would swear meant, "Yeah, I'm a *cat*."

And then he went back to sleep. He was now centered on the pillow, although I had never seen him move over to flow into my space.

Well, it wasn't like I had been planning to go back to sleep, anyway.

I found my shoes and art bag under the chair that was now in its customary place under the east-facing window and not against the door. Then I went out into the hall and found the open door of the bathroom.

One quick face wash later, and I was feeling immeasurably better. I hadn't gotten the long sleep I had been hoping for, but it was more than I had expected to get when we'd gone into Esja's bedroom the night before. I would take it.

The humidity was starting to tick up again, I could tell by the insane curling of my red hair. But I gathered it up as best I could and pinned it up off my neck. Then I headed downstairs in search of the others.

I found Nilda first, still dressed from her guard duty and smelling faintly of bonfire smoke. She was standing at the counter in the kitchen, peering into the contents of the coffee carafe.

"There's enough for one," she said without looking up, as if she knew it was me by the sound of my footsteps. Which, yeah. She and her sister both had a heavy stride, and Esja flitted about like a ghost. I guessed I was pretty distinctive being in the middle of those two extremes.

"You can have it," I said.

"No, I shouldn't. I need to get some sleep, and coffee isn't going to help with that," she said. She poured the last of the coffee into a mug from the cabinet, then handed it to me. "There are cinnamon rolls and a fruit salad on the table. Kara didn't quite eat everything but the honeydew."

"Thanks," I said, taking the mug from her, then snatching up one of the cinnamon rolls. "Where are Kara and Esja?"

"In the garden," Nilda said around an enormous yawn. "Kara filled me in on last night. What are we going to do? If your grandmother's spells can't even make her keep a promise?"

"There's something going on, but I'm going to get to the bottom of it," I said.

And in the bright light of day, that actually felt doable. Or maybe it was just the amount of sleep I had gotten. Either way, my head felt clearer, and while I hadn't had a single dream, let alone one with hints of a solution, I was able to think clearly enough to come up with a few options on my own.

"Kara said she isn't leaving Esja's side until I'm up to relieve her, so I better hit the sack," Nilda said, struggling to stifle yet another yawn. "Wake me if you need me. I mean it."

"We will," I promised her.

I ate half the cinnamon roll in two bites, then carried the rest along with the mug of coffee out to the Mikkelsens' front garden.

Kara was sitting in a garden chair placed not too subtly right in front of the gate that opened onto the street. Although anyone who was willing to climb out of windows would surely be undeterred by the idea of vaulting a fence.

But Esja in the morning light didn't look like a flight risk. In fact, she looked more like her old self than I had expected. Not that she was thin and pale like before. She was still the bloom of good health with color to her cheeks and golden, sun-kissed skin.

But she was dressed in the sort of clothes I was more used to seeing her wear: a simple linen underdress of a cornflower blue that matched her eyes with an apron-dress over it of what had once been snowy-white.

That apron dress was now more dapples of paint than original white from where simple brooches pinned the shoulder straps to where it ended just below her knees.

She didn't always wear the same apron dress when she was painting, but only because she had two. This one was linen like her underdress, cooler for summer painting. Her other was wool. But both were equally decorated in splashes of paint.

Which had to be deliberate. I had seen Esja paint before, and never once had I ever seen her drip or splash. She worked carefully, meticulously, always in complete control of her paint and water both.

Yeah, I admit, I was a little jealous. Watercolors were not my favorite medium.

But it's not like pen and ink didn't have its own challenges.

"Good morning, Ingrid," Esja said from behind her easel as she saw me standing in the shade of the doorway. "Or is it afternoon?"

"Still morning," Kara said from her perch on the chair.

"Barely," I admitted, and took another bite of cinnamon roll. Then I circled around Esja so I could see what she was painting.

She had found the corner of the Mikkelsens' garden where the chives were in fullest bloom. There appeared to be a few varieties planted there, as I saw a range of blossoms from deep purple to lighter pink to white.

Two more paintings were laid out in the shade of the front porch, although the paint on both looked quite dry now. One was of the pear tree that grew in the far corner of the garden, and the other was of the house itself, the windows all brightly illuminated by the rising sun.

"You've been up for a while," I said.

"I'm not really a late sleeper. Even if I'm up late," she hastened to add. As if I might take offense.

"Can you take a break for a moment? I want to talk to you," I said.

"Of course," Esja said, and carefully washed her brush before setting it down to dry. At my gesture, she followed me back to the porch and sat beside me on the step.

"Esja, what do *you* think is going on?" I asked her.

"I'm sorry to cause so much trouble and worry," she said. "I really don't mean to."

"But you keep sneaking out at night. That's the worrying thing," I said.

"I'm just going out to see people. That's all," she said.

"Esja, you're *sneaking out* to see people. That's different. If you don't think anything you're doing is wrong, why are you being so sneaky about it?"

She chewed at her lip, then just shrugged. "I don't know."

"That's not an answer," Kara said wearily from her chair across the garden.

"Have you had any odd dreams lately?" I asked her.

"What do you mean?" Esja asked with a frown.

"Have you dreamed you were talking to anyone or anything? Or going somewhere like on a journey? Or even just picking something up?" I asked. "Anything out of the ordinary at all."

"I sometimes dream I'm back in my house and that my brother is there, but I wake up before I can find him," Esja said. "It's not a nightmare or anything. Just a pretty standard dream. I mean, I *am* always wondering where he is."

"I suppose," I said. A magic-infused dream would stand out. If she had had one, she'd know it. She wouldn't have to question it. The difference between that and a normal dream was pretty stark.

Of course, there was always the possibility she wasn't being honest with me.

But her wide blue eyes were as sincere as ever.

"And it goes without saying you haven't done any of those things in your waking life, either?" I asked. "You've not spoken with any strangers or gone for any walks in the woods?"

"No one but you and the Thors go into the woods," Esja said.

Which wasn't strictly speaking true.

Kara was thinking the same thing, as she put in, "And your brother."

"Of course. My brother," Esja said. "But I wouldn't do that. Loke has always been very clear that the woods are full of things better avoided. Anyway, I'm not very outdoorsy. Being in this garden since I've come into the village has been outside enough for me."

"She does come out to paint nearly every day," Kara said. She caught my eye and touched her own cheek, as if telling me that she knew where Esja had gotten her suntan.

I gave her the smallest of nods, but kept my attention on Esja. Whose eyes were still wide and sincere.

"Did you want to draw me?" Esja asked.

"Actually, I'm going to walk back to your house and take a closer look at things there," I said. "Do I have your permission to go inside?"

"Of course," Esja said. "I don't know what you'll find there, but my life is an open book to you, Ingrid. I don't know why you all think something is going on, but I'll do whatever you want me to if it will help you feel better about things. And I remember my promises." She touched three fingertips to her forehead and smiled at me.

"You didn't remember last night," Kara said.

"She'll remember now," I said, patting Esja on the knee.

Then I got up and walked over to the gate. Kara got up from her chair but didn't move it, just waited for me to get close enough for the two of us to have a whispered conversation.

"Why don't you just draw her?" she asked.

"What do you think it will show me that we haven't seen already? If there's one thing we've been examining super closely, it's Esja herself," I said.

"You've already drawn the house," she said, her frown deepening.

"Just the outside. Maybe the inside will have more clues," I said. Before Kara could argue, I went on. "That's not all I'm going to be checking out, though. It's just all I'm sharing with Esja."

"You have a plan?" Kara asked, finally perking up a little.

"I have part of a plan," I said. "At least, I have some things I want to check out, and I hope if I learn anything, it will lead to a plan."

"I was thinking about our conversation from before," Kara said. "If Esja is toggling between two states, and there's no point in checking her for magic when she's in her current state, maybe I should hang close to her and watch for her to change. Then look at her again."

"No, don't do that," I said.

"I'll be better prepared this time," she said.

"It still might be too much, and if you're incapacitated again, it might be bad," I said. "Just stay close to her, but if she changes, call Mormor and me. We'll get to you as quick as we can, and the three of us can look at Esja in her altered state."

"She was different yesterday morning," Kara said, whispering even more quietly than before, and moving closer to me so that even if Esja was looking our way and could read lips—which I didn't think she could—she wouldn't be able to see what Kara was saying. "As different as she is when she's entertaining the crowd in the mead hall, when she came home yesterday morning and started throwing her fit, she was very different. *Very* different."

"I believe you," I said. "It's the only thing that explains how she broke her promise to Mormor. That she was, somehow, very different when she left last night. But I feel like she won't be that different so long as I'm here, watching her. That's why I'm asking you to call for us if you see that again. Because you're the one most likely to see it."

"I will call for you," she said with obvious reluctance. Only then did she start pulling her chair out of the way so I could open the gate.

But she stopped me just as I was lifting the latch, resting a hand on mine as she said, "Ingrid? Don't go far."

"I'll be in Villmark the whole time. If I think I have to go farther, I'll see you first and let you know. Okay?"

She bit at her lip, but nodded and let my hand go.

I headed towards the main north-south road through town, and took a right turn to go south, towards the farms and towards Loke's and Esja's house.

And tried to stifle the feeling that, as much as I really did hope to find some kind of clue there, what I was really doing was delaying the inevitable.

But the lead I intended to follow up on after that was not going to be a pleasant interview. It never was, talking with Halldis.

My only comfort was I really honestly believed she had nothing to do with what was going on.

But she might know.

Might. And I doubted she would tell me more than she wanted me to know.

And there'd be her usual gloating and speaking in loud subtext.

It couldn't be avoided. But I could delay it, if only for an hour.

CHAPTER FOURTEEN

ᚺ

THE HOUSE, as expected, told me nothing.

Although being able to go inside it without feeling like an intruder, at least I got that nothing from some new angles. So there was that. But my sketches all just looked like sketches of rooms of a house. I saw nothing in pencil or charcoal that looked like anything in particular.

It had definitely been the center of the hailstorm. But I still couldn't say if that was because something making itself a target had drawn the storm there, or if something in hunter mode had directed it there, or if the whole thing was just a coincidence.

If only it were possible to go to where the storm had formed out over the lake and draw things from that angle.

Well, there were boats to be had. It wasn't such a terrible idea.

But in that moment, it felt like one delay too many from what I had to do next.

And so I found myself in the meadow beyond the bluffs over-looking Runde, descending the natural stone stairway down to the caverns below.

The day had gotten sticky and hot while I had been walking south then back again, and the cool interior of the caves was a welcome relief, if still a rather damp one.

If Nilda and Kara were both home, that meant it was Valki tending the ancestral fire again. But since I was heading for the deeper caves, I wasn't going in his direction. I could see the flickering light from the fire even through the turn in the cave between that cavern and this larger one where all the caves met, but that was all.

I wasn't entirely surprised when I turned towards the cave that spiraled down into the depths to find Mjolner there, waiting for me. He could be protective that way.

"You know where I'm going," I said to him.

He gave me a slow blink, then led the way into the darkness.

I turned on the flashlight on my cellphone, then followed behind him.

Halldis' cell was sealed by a stone, a boulder so heavy only the Thors could move it.

Of course, there was more than one way around a rock. Loke could just step through it, with his strange power of teleporting via doorways. Apparently, a rock blocking the mouth of a cave was enough like a doorway for his power to work on it. Perhaps because it had been deliberately placed to serve as a door.

But Loke was far in the north.

Still, I had other ways at my disposal.

"Lead on," I said to Mjolner. He had come to a stop before the stone and was wiping at one of his ears. Not a full-on wash, more like some bit of something was bothering him. But he finished off with a flick of his paw, then looked up at me.

He slow-blinked his lamp-bright eyes at me.

And I found myself slow-blinking back.

And in that blink, I just moved through the stone, like I was being pulled through water by some strange current.

When I opened my eyes, I was at the top of a tunnel that looked like it had been formed by some huge stone-eating worm, the sides perfectly round but in ridges like I was standing inside something's ribcage.

It spiraled down, a tighter spiral than the larger cave I had just come from. But at the bottom, there was a flickering of firelight.

Mjolner sat down in his most formal pose, tail wrapped around his six-toed paws, and held his head up high.

Halldis couldn't tolerate his presence, so he was going to wait here. But he was going to be a watchful waiter. Not even a quick cat bath was going to distract him if I needed him.

I gave him a silent nod, to tell him I understood.

Then I took a single step, my sneaker soundless on the dusty floor. But I wasn't entirely surprised to hear Halldis call up, "Well met, Ingrid Torfudottir. I've been waiting for you."

"Have you?" I countered as I strode down the spiral cave to the squared-off cavern that was her prison home. Her round wooden table set with two chairs just to the left of the bottom of the cave.

The bookshelf free of spell books or even vaguely useful nonfiction beside an overstuffed but comfortable-looking reading chair with a modern adjustable light curved over the back of it to illuminate the lap of the reader. Who wasn't there at the moment.

The bed on the far side piled high with wool blankets. It may be another sticky August day above, but down here, the temperature was always on the chilly side, and the dampness never abated. Not even the fire crackling merrily in the fireplace that spanned most of the length of the wall to my right did much to dispel that cool dampness.

It seemed a casual observation to me, but something had me stopping mid stride, had me paying more attention to that fireplace.

The last time I had been here, it had been doing the job of keeping the large space warm and dry.

But then, the last time I had been here, that fire had clearly been fueled by magic.

Now I could see a half-empty woodbox that hadn't been there before. And fresh logs on the fire, threatening to stifle the flames that were there before those flames got a hold on their own wood, the way logs sometimes did.

"I have to cook food as well," Halldis said drily, and my eyes scanned the room until they finally found her. She was in a little nook tucked behind the curve of the spiral cave's wall. There was a little table there, a workspace to judge by the generous dusting of flour all over its surface. Two shelves were hung over it, each holding a variety of canisters. Those canisters were a matched set of glazed pottery with neatly fitted covers, but not a one of them had a label.

But Halldis herself was standing there facing me with a bowl in her arms. It was covered by a clean kitchen towel, but to judge by the yeasty smell in the air, it contained dough she had just finished kneading.

She carried it across the room to the hearth and set it on the stones close enough for it to stay warm, but not too warm. Then she picked up a poker and tried to get the logs to cooperate.

The sleeves of her underdress were rolled up past her elbows, probably for the kneading she had just finished. There was certainly flour there, clinging to her pale skin.

But that wasn't what had me staring.

She looked terrible. And that was absolutely shocking.

The idea that she could no longer use her magic to keep her prison home warm and comfortable, or to magic up whatever food she most wanted without expending any mundane sort of effort, was one thing.

But to have let all of her glamor drop? That could only mean one thing.

She had lost all of her magic entirely. Whatever source she had been drawing on despite all my grandmother's wards and the protective power of these caves themselves, that was all gone now.

Unless this was another play for pity. She had tried that before, when all of her bad deeds had caught up with her and the council—but mainly my grandmother dispensing justice as volva—had condemned her to this cell. She had dropped her appearance of youthful glow and sensual beauty. She had looked like a shrunken crone, with a shriveled, crooked spine and a face like a dried crabapple.

It hadn't worked. No one had felt pity for her.

And the idea that she thought it would move me to pity now? I, who had been in the thralls of her power, if only for a moment? I had more reason than most to hate her.

There was no way she thought she could provoke pity in me. No, this had to be real.

"Where has your magic gone, Halldis?" I asked her directly.

She scoffed, but said nothing. So her attitude was as strong as ever.

But I couldn't ignore the obvious parallel. Esja had gained in strength and health while Halldis had withered away.

Was there a connection?

"I would ask why it mattered, keeping up appearance when I get so few visitors. But this is a bit of a banner day," she said, still poking at the fire.

"You don't want to flash even a little bit of glamor my way?" I asked her.

She didn't answer. But the logs she was poking at finally burst into bright flame. She put the poker back in its place in the fireplace tool rack, then turned to face me as she rolled her sleeves back down to her bony wrists.

"The power you swore yourself to has abandoned you, Halldis," I said. "Don't you want to tell me about it now? Even just a hint? I know you thrive on revenge."

"You know nothing, Torfudottir," she said, but without her usual venom.

"Educate me," I said.

She scoffed out a quick laugh at that, but I sensed this was more at her own expense than at mine. But whatever her thoughts were, she gave me no hint of them.

"Can you sense the weather, down here?" I asked her, trying for as casual a tone as I could.

But she wasn't fooled. "I can sense hailstorms when they're booming loud with magic, yes. But that's nothing to do with me. Not anymore."

She sounded wistful, if only for an instant. Then she quickly turned away, as if she didn't want me to see what was in her eyes.

A moment of weakness? I doubted it. And yet, I had to try.

"Do you really plan to just waste away down here until the end of your days? And the thing that has abandoned you here just goes on like it's nothing?" I asked her.

"I wouldn't call it a *thing* if I were you," she said darkly.

"What should I call it?" I asked.

"You shouldn't speak of it at all," she said. "It's not for the likes of you."

"You don't think I can handle the power?" I asked, and realized I was flexing my hand a little. I was making Kara with her hand on her sword look downright subtle.

But if Halldis felt like I was threatening her with magic, she didn't acknowledge it. She just scoffed out another tired little laugh.

"You couldn't handle the darkness," she said.

"But you could," I said.

"Not just me, little volva," she said, finally looking up at me. Her face might be shriveled and wrinkled beyond recognition, but her eyes were as sharp and dangerous as ever. "You won't want to believe it, but it's not just me."

"I find I can believe almost anything these days," I told her.

She quirked a single eyebrow at me but said nothing.

"Did you make a bargain with something from the north or something from the lake?" I asked.

She blinked in surprise, then quickly looked away again. Like she knew her face kept betraying her.

But her words when she spoke them were as strongly determined as ever. "You might be getting closer to asking the right questions, but it won't help you in the end. You are not ready for this fight. You never will be. It's not meant to *be* your fight."

"Whose fight is it, then?" I asked her.

She said nothing.

"This bargain you made—" I started again.

But she spun to face me. In the blink of an eye, she was toe to toe with me. Although shrunken as she was, she had to get up on tiptoe to stare up into my face.

Still, that burst of preternatural speed? She had some power left in her. Whether she knew it or not.

"Yes, a bargain. Do you take me for a fool? I made a bargain with a being, but I understood every part of that situation. I knew myself. I knew the being. I knew the bargain itself. And all that has transpired since has been exactly as I knew it could be."

"Not *would* be?" I asked her.

"This," she said, ignoring my question to wave her arms around and encompass her prison home. "This is all one of the many possibilities of the bargain I swore to. I have not been tricked. I have not been played false. You will not sway me to your side with talk of revenge. I have nothing to seek revenge for."

"This was the price, then?" I asked her.

She made a noncommittal sound, not quite yes, but not quite no. But she had shrunk back down into herself, and her eyes no longer met mine.

"I can't say I'm sorry to see you like this," I told her as I headed back to the cave. I had had enough of this place and this conversation both.

"Yes, you are," she said to me. This time, when she laughed, it wasn't a self-directed scoff. It was a cackle.

At my expense.

"What's so funny?" I asked her. Although I really didn't think it was wise. Never feed the trolls, right? She wanted me to ask. And I'd just given her what she wanted.

But she just cackled again. "You are sorry to see me like this. Because you've seen the reverse, haven't you? And that is going to eat at your mind for a long, long time."

"What do you know about it?" I demanded.

But she just settled back into her reading chair, hands on her bony knees, and cackled away.

I doubted there would be an end to her hysterical laughter any time soon.

Or any honest answers to my questions when she was done.

And Mjolner was meowing at me from the top of the cave. If my cat was telling me it was time to go, it was definitely time to go.

"You know, you'd get more visitors if you made any effort to be helpful," I said to her.

But she just laughed all the harder, wiping at the deepest corners of her eyes.

I let Mjolner's magic carry me back into the blessed silence of the cave on the other side of the stone, but I felt like I could still sense that laughter in my mind.

She knew about Esja. I was certain of it.

But how did she know?

And why was she taking it with such high spirits? Because I couldn't see a single thing she had to gain from her power leaving her in favor of another.

And yet, I knew imagining the possibilities was going to be my nightmare fuel for a long time to come.

CHAPTER FIFTEEN

I DIDN'T GO BACK UP to the surface right away. I took a moment first, out of Halldis' sight if not her actual perceptions, and took out my bronze wand. I waved it before my eyes until it was a shiny blur and let my vision unfocus.

I no longer needed to do this to see the flow of magic around me, of course. But it made the transition faster and my magical perception stronger when I did it this way. Not quite as strong as if my grandmother had been there with me, but pretty close.

And Mjolner was there beside me. I think he was helping too. But his magic was still a mystery to me. Maybe all he offered was moral support.

But whatever. It helped. I could see the patterns in the stones around me stronger than I usually did.

The wards my grandmother had placed all around Halldis's cell stood as strongly woven as ever. I would be able to see signs if Halldis had been so much as testing their limits, like an animal messing with an electric fence, but there were none. She was waiting out her time inside that cell, quietly and passively.

And nothing on the outside was trying to get in.

I looked more deeply at the patterns of the stones themselves. These weren't ordinary stone. Nothing this close to the source of my ancestor Torfa's power was ordinary. But there was no sign of anyone tapping into that power, or passing any power through it.

Halldis had probably heard the storm passing overhead. She was deep underground, but not so deep that thunder wouldn't reach her ears.

But that didn't explain how she seemed to know about Esja.

Unless she hadn't. Like most charlatans, she was highly skilled with cold reading. She had known I'd come down there for some reason. She could just be very good at guessing what that reason might be.

And what she had said hadn't been so specific it couldn't be a guess.

It wasn't even that big of a leap of inference. I was sure my shock at her appearance had shown on my face. I wasn't very good at hiding things when I was feeling them, I knew that for a fact.

It was all too likely that she had seen not just shock on my face, but also a hint of the worry I had for Esja. I mean, I'd been thinking about her. The irony, the paradox of their parallel but reversed paths.

Or maybe I was missing the obvious. She might be cooking her own food and warming herself by burning wood, but that only meant someone was bringing her those things. She couldn't create them magically, or she'd just be making fire instead of firewood.

I toyed with the idea of talking to Valki about it, but what would his confirmation actually tell me? Even if I knew who was in charge of bringing her things, it was either himself, a Mikkelsen, or a Thor.

And I trusted all of those people with my entire life.

If Halldis was getting knowledge of the happenings in Villmark from any of them, it was against their will. And no one knew better than I the many ways she could trick you into revealing things to her. Often without even realizing you had.

Besides, I was getting an itch in the back of my brain. I needed to check in with Esja. It was the middle of the afternoon, too early to hit the mead halls. But it was about the time that Kara and Nilda would be trading off their guard duty of her.

If she really were possessed by something malevolent, that would be the moment for it to act.

I hurried my steps, then broke into a run.

Which lasted until I climbed the stairs up to the meadow and the full blast of thick, humid, nauseatingly hot air smothered me.

There was no way I was going to keep running in that.

Even just walking at a faster than normal clip had me bathed in sweat before I had even started down the path that wound through the stands of birch trees between the meadow and the eastern edge of the village.

I wasn't the only one repulsed by the weather, apparently. Despite being the middle of the afternoon, few were moving around in Villmark. I wasn't far enough south to see the marketplace, and there was probably still some activity there. But in the streets lined with homes and across the expanse of the village commons, there was no sign of anyone about. I occasionally heard the sound of a cranky child likely protesting the heat, but that was all. Not even the dogs were barking.

So it was a bit of a surprise to come in through the garden gate to see Esja still outside. Kara had said she spent most of her time out there, painting, but I guess I had thought she had only meant when the weather was tolerable.

When I came in, she was sitting on the chair that Kara had vacated. It was no longer blocking the path of the gate, but it was still positioned with its back to me.

I turned to push the gate closed behind me, but even as I did so, my brain started highlighting a few things I had just seen without really noticing.

To start with, Esja had taken off her wide-brimmed hat, which didn't seem wise. She was now in the middle of the garden, far from any shade. She had to be burning her skin, tanned or not.

She had also been turned at an awkward angle in that chair, looking back over her shoulder at me with a bright, merry gleam to her eyes.

That couldn't be what was causing my growing sense of alarm. Could it?

Well, lately, Esja looking merry *was* a bit of an alarming situation.

I was still looking at my own hand pushing the latch of the gate closed, puzzling it all over, when the last bit of information slotted into place.

She had been looking back at me over her *bare* shoulder. I had seen her skin down past the bottom of her shoulder blades. All deeply tanned. Not new, that tan.

And while I had yet to see anyone in a bikini anywhere in Villmark, I hadn't even seen that much sign of clothing on Esja.

I resisted the urge to spin back around. It was actually stiflingly hot enough where such a dramatic move might leave me lightheaded after my long, water-less walk all over town.

I slowly pivoted on the heels of my sneakers until I was facing Esja again.

Who was still looking at me over her naked shoulder. Her hair was loose, gathered together and pulled forward over her other shoulder. But she had pretty thin hair, thin and very lightly colored.

I doubted it covered much.

"Esja. What are we doing?" I asked her.

"Don't move, kjær. I haven't finished yet." A man's voice.

That was when I realized that we weren't alone. And it wasn't either Kara or Nilda who was in the garden with us.

It was Skefill. He was standing just where I had left Esja that morning. Standing at her very easel, in fact. Painting with her paints.

And wearing her hat. I'm not sure why that particular detail jumped out at me.

I wished I could say it made him look silly. But it didn't. He had rolled the brim a bit, perhaps that did it. But mostly he looked like Vincent Van Gogh, if Van Gogh had let his beard grow to Viking lengths.

"What is going on here?" I asked in a fierce whisper. Like I was afraid of disturbing something about the moment.

Maybe I did. There was a stifling feeling about the whole situation that wasn't coming from the weather. It was more like something else, something not remotely like a storm, was about to break.

But Esja just laughed. I could tell she was trying not to move; most of that laughter was in her eyes.

"I'm properly covered, Ingrid," she said to me. "Skefill is just painting my portrait. Just a little innocent making of art."

"In direct sunlight?" I asked.

"That's what I said," Skefill said as he leaned in to touch the brush to the painting. I could see the tip of his tongue just poking out from between his teeth as he focused on his task.

"That's what he always says," Esja mock whispered at me and rolled her eyes.

Great. They'd done this before. I guess this explained her apparently all-over tan. Modeling for figure drawing.

"Esja, how are you feeling right now?" I asked her.

"I'm fine. I'm me," she said, moving to sit a little higher in the chair, to look at me more directly.

Skefill made a sound of protest, gesturing at the painting in front of him.

"Skefill, love, I'm afraid we're done for the day," Esja said as she got up from the chair, sliding her arms back into the sleeves of her under-dress and lacing it back up before turning to face me.

But I walked right past her. I needed to see what Skefill had been painting.

On a couple of levels, actually.

"It's a work in progress," he said when he saw me marching over to him. But at my harsh glare, he stepped back, raising his hands as if in total surrender as he made room for me to examine his painting.

Which, I had to admit, was actually really good. Not finished, that's true. He had intended to frame Esja's form with the garden plants behind her. They were lightly penciled in, but only a first blocking in layer of color had been applied to them.

Still, those touches of green were enough to offset the more fully rendered golden tones of Esja's skin. In his portrait, her hair was thicker and fuller and longer, covering enough of her top half to be decent.

He hadn't painted her dress at all, just her legs turned sideways, the knee of the forward leg pulled up to rest against the arm of the chair. I didn't think she'd been sitting that way, but I didn't know she hadn't.

"You can't be mad about this," Esja said as she suddenly appeared at Skefill's other shoulder. She, too, looked at the portrait and made a soft ooh of appreciation. "This is your best one yet."

"I didn't get to finish," he said, but released the brush in his hand when she touched it. She washed the brush clean of paint, then set it with her others.

"I'm not mad, Esja," I said, rubbing at my forehead. "I'm just confused. This doesn't seem like you."

"And yet, I'm me," she insisted. She looked up at Skefill, noticed her hat, and took it back from him, carefully smoothing down her hair before setting it in place. "I'm still me."

I searched her for signs of magic again, and again saw nothing.

I opened my mouth to express all of my thousand worries, but was all too aware of Skefill still standing there, listening.

"Skefill, art time is over. It's time for you to go," I said, gesturing towards the garden gate.

"I don't jump at your bidding," he said darkly. His hand made a little move that I was all too familiar with. Reaching for the hilt of a weapon.

Which wasn't there. But he played it cool, setting it instead on his hip as if that was what he had intended the entire time.

"Your things are just over there," Esja whispered to him. There was just a hint of laughing mischief in her voice, but when she saw me watching her, she shifted back to wide-eyed innocence. "Of course, I always prefer painting with you, Ingrid. But you're so busy."

That refrain was growing tiresome, but I let it go. I knew the heat was making me cranky, and being snotty with her wasn't going to help anything.

"I won't go unless you ask me to," Skefill said to Esja. "If she is bullying you, if the Mikkelsens are bullying you, I'll take you away from here. You don't have to stay. I can protect you. I'll keep you safe."

I had a thousand responses to that, but none of them mattered.

I wanted to know what Esja had to say.

She gazed up at him with her big blue eyes, like he was her entire world.

And if *I* was feeling that, I could only imagine what it felt like for him on the receiving end.

But she just put her hand on his arm and said, "I'm perfectly fine. As I keep telling you. As I keep telling *everyone*. But thank you for saying that. It is lovely to hear."

"I meant every word," he said. He started to dip his head towards her, but she stepped back at the last moment, spinning away as if she were dancing again.

Spinning to her next partner.

For a minute, Skefill just stood there. I watched, fascinated, as his face shifted from one angry, dumbfounded color to the next.

But then he closed his eyes, took a deep breath, and pulled himself together.

He opened his eyes and gave me an inscrutable look. Then he turned, picked up his sword and axe where he had left them on the front porch, and headed towards the garden gate.

I was just turning to Esja to suggest we go inside, out of the sun, when she dashed down the paved garden path to catch Skefill at the gate. He had taken a step out into the street, but she easily stopped him with her hand on his arm again.

He looked down at that hand, like her softest touch was a sensation worth dying for.

Then she was in his arms entirely, pressing up against him as she planted the briefest of kisses on his mouth. He was clearly too shocked to respond, and she was gone again, skipping back to the house before he had quite realized what was happening.

He almost had my pity.

Almost.

Esja gave me a dazzling smile when she'd rejoined me, catching onto both of my hands in hers like we were the oldest of childhood friends.

"I think he might be my favorite," she said, her eyes bright.

Then I had a little taste of what Skefill must be feeling when she was just gone, disappeared from my grasp and already inside the house.

And still, when I looked, there wasn't a bit of magic to her.

CHAPTER SIXTEEN

ᚺ

I FOLLOWED Esja inside to find both Mikkelsen sisters sitting together at the kitchen table. Nilda was downing a huge mug of black coffee, and Kara was eying that coffee with real envy.

"Skefill comes over a lot, I'm guessing?" I said to the two of them as I watched Esja dance over to the icebox and dig out a pitcher of iced tea.

"Does he?" Kara said, blinking.

"He was here just now," I said, gesturing towards the front garden. "And you weren't with Esja. Neither of you were."

"I don't need a babysitter," Esja said, even as she poured too much iced tea into her glass and spilled all over the Mikkelsens' counter. She set the pitcher back in the icebox, then grabbed a towel to dab up the mess.

"I was," Kara said, but she sounded sleepy and confused. "No, I came inside. I was getting lightheaded in the heat. I'm sorry. I wasn't thinking."

Nilda and I both looked at her with real concern. She was looking both pale and flushed at once. Blotchy, I guess you'd call it.

"I'm feeling better now," she said. But I went and fetched her a glass of the iced tea, anyway.

Then I poured another for myself. I needed to do a better job of staying hydrated, especially when I was running around town all day.

"Skefill has been here before?" I asked again after downing half of my glass in one long swallow.

"Yes, he has," Esja said. She didn't join us at the table but remained standing, leaning against the counter as she rubbed the condensation on the outside of her glass across her sweaty forehead. "He comes over to paint with me."

"I think I remember that," Kara said.

"I thought that Esja was spending most of her time alone out in the garden, but if she had visitors, no one would've objected," Nilda said.

"We need to get more help on the patrols, don't we?" I said, looking at the two of them, both of them bleary-eyed and desperately trying to focus on me. "And I don't just mean the patrols of the borders of the village. I was just down in the caves, having a little chat with Halldis. A pointless waste of time, but I did notice Valki was alone with no second to aid him if there were any trouble. No one is guarding the fire but the two of you and Valki. Am I right?"

"There's usually a Thor in the mix," Nilda said. "Depending on which one is in town at the moment. But otherwise, yeah. The three of us."

"That's too many shifts and not enough down time. I know guarding the fire sounds like an easy task, but I also know it isn't. There's more to it than staring into the flames," I said.

"It's draining, staying on alert," Kara said.

"I'll bring it up with the council," I said.

"Valki is a third of the council," Nilda pointed out. "If he wanted more help, he'd already have it."

"You're working too hard, and I won't hear any argument otherwise," I said.

Then I looked at Esja again. "Who else visits you in the garden?"

"I'm allowed to have friends," she said stubbornly.

"Of course you are," I readily agreed. "Who?"

"Raggi," she said. Which I had pretty much guessed already.

Then she said a name I absolutely hadn't. "Roarr."

"Roarr?" I repeated. "He's never at Aldís's mead hall. Is he?"

"I don't meet him in the mead hall. I talk to him in the garden while I'm painting," Esja said. As if that were the most obvious thing in the world.

"About what?" I asked.

"Just things," she said. "He knows Loke is in the north, and he just stops by to see how I'm doing. It's just friendly."

"I feel like we should've been more aware of all this," Kara said to Nilda.

"Nothing is going on," Esja said. "I wasn't being sneaky. You guys are always busy. Busy or sleeping. Because you're busy at night."

"These men aren't busy?" I asked.

"Sure they are," Esja said. "They all take shifts patrolling the perimeter of Villmark. But they also make time to see me."

"And Skefill is your favorite," I said.

Kara looked startled at that, but Esja just laughed.

"I said I *think* he *might* be. But I'm not in any hurry to make a decision," she said.

"Make a decision about what?" Kara asked.

"Come on," Esja said. "As much as I appreciate you letting me stay with you, and Sigvin too, I can't live with you all forever. And I definitely don't want to go back to that house."

Kara shot me a questioning look, but I shook my head and shrugged at the same time. I had found nothing at the house. But given the state it was in and how isolated it was, it wasn't hard to understand why Esja wouldn't want to go back there.

"You're looking for a husband?" Nilda asked, aghast.

"You say that like it's weird," Esja said.

"I don't think your brother is going to take it well if he comes back to find you wed and gone," Nilda said.

"I'm not *leaving*," Esja said. "I'll still be in Villmark. Just in a different house."

"If it was suitors you were looking for, you could've asked us," Kara said.

"And you would do what?" Esja asked. "Not to be mean, but you don't have any brothers. Or male cousins. Or anything."

"I have some very impressive brothers-in-law," Kara said with half a smile. "Granted, one is taken," she added with a nod in my direction.

"I think what we need here is naps all around until the heat breaks, and then dinner at my grandmother's mead hall," I said. "Esja can mingle with that crowd."

"If she falls for a Runde guy, Loke really will kill us," Nilda said.

"Nonsense. If anyone spends more time in Runde than I do, it's Loke. Under normal circumstances, anyway," I belatedly added.

A quiet fell over the room. We could hear the insects droning in the heat outside the house, but nothing more.

"I'm going to get that nap," Kara said at last, setting her empty glass in the sink, then heading for the stairs.

"I'm all wired from that coffee," Nilda said, looking down at her empty mug. "I think I'll go talk to Valki, see if we can't get a Thor to watch the fire tonight. I would rather all three of us stayed close to Esja if we're taking her out tonight."

"I don't *need* a babysitter," Esja protested again, but we both ignored her.

"I'll stay here with her," I said to Nilda. She nodded, put her own mug in the sink, then headed out the front door.

After I heard the sound of the garden gate latching behind her, I turned my attention to Esja.

"I don't need a nap," she said the minute she felt my eyes on her. "I'm perfectly okay."

"That's not what I was about to say," I told her.

"What *were* you going to say?" she asked.

"I was just going to offer to send for Loke," I said. "You're clearly going through some things, and if you need your brother here, I understand. Mjolner can find him, no matter where he is. And Loke and Mjolner always understand each other. I don't know how, they just do. If you need your brother, I can tell him so. If you want me to."

To my surprise, my offer brought tears to Esja's eyes. She fell into the chair that Kara had been sitting in and collapsed against the table, burying her face in her hands. But she didn't sob. She just sat quietly for a moment.

Then she raised her face and lowered her hands. Her tears were gone, but her face was red and blotchy.

"Esja?" I said.

"I want to see him. So badly. But I know I can't. Whatever he's doing, he wouldn't have gone away if it wasn't really, really important. And nothing that I'm feeling now is more important than that," she said.

"You should tell him everything. Write it all down. Then Mjolner can take your message to him. Let him be the judge of what's more important," I said.

"No, I can't do that," she said, firmly shaking her head. "He would come right back. That wouldn't mean it was more important. It's just what he would do. I'm sorry you think I'm a mess right now. I'll try harder to be… normal, I guess. But don't tell him anything. Please, just don't."

"Don't make any engagements without talking to him," I said.

"I won't," she said with a laugh. "Honestly, I'm still trying to meet as many people as I can. Everything is so new. I don't see myself really wanting to settle down anytime soon. But I do miss Loke. And this does help pass the time."

I nodded, but her words weren't quite enough to put my heart at ease.

"Look, if neither of us are napping before dinnertime, do you want to draw me now?" she asked.

"Yes," I said, pushing away from the kitchen table. "I would like that very much."

We settled outside, but in the shade of the porch. Esja arranged herself just so on the cast-iron bench to the left of the front door. She had clearly been doing a bit of posing for Skefill. She knew what positions she could hold long enough for someone else to commit them to paper.

I drew her in pencils, as she sat with her knees drawn up to her chest, head tipped back against the back of the bench, looking pensive. Almost wistful.

I thought, when I was done, that there were a few Hagall runes in the woodwork from the house exterior that I had sketched in behind her. But that was it. There was nothing else there but a young woman who didn't quite know what to do with herself. She had so much energy and so little guidance about what she should be doing with it.

"You should think about hosting art lessons," I said as I added a last touch of shading to her hair in the portrait.

"Have Skefill bring some friends?" she asked with a smile.

"I was thinking of the kids in Villmark, but no one is ever too old to learn art," I said.

She sat up at that, her feet hitting the porch with a thump as she leaned forward to look at me. "You're serious. You think I can teach art?"

"Certainly," I said. "Well, it's worth trying, anyway. Not everyone who can do a thing is good at teaching it. But even if you don't like teaching, just hosting an informal gathering of other artists might be fun for you. Like a salon or something."

"I never thought of that," she said.

"You've been hanging with Raggi, Skefill and Roarr, but you never thought of finding other people to hang out with?" I asked.

"Well," she said slowly, her cheeks coloring ever so slightly. "Those were the ones who stopped by to see me. That's how I know them. I never invited anybody."

"Oh," I said. I was starting to get the picture. Esja had been lonely, but she'd also been lacking in the skills to know how to remedy that situation. She had just sat alone, lamenting how busy all the people she already knew were, and wished for more.

"But I'm going to meet more people tonight, right?" she asked.

"Absolutely," I said.

"I can't wait," she said. "Do you mind if I go upstairs and clean up before we go? I've been sweating all day and I think I stink."

"No jumping out the window?" I asked. Not quite joking.

But she answered me with a smile. "No jumping out the window. I'll only be a minute."

I nodded my consent, and she dashed into the house, running up the stairs with all the energy of a child.

She really was healthier than I'd ever seen her. Although it bothered me that I still didn't know why. Was it important? If she was better, wasn't that enough?

I had been all over her house. If anything there had been cursed, I would've sensed it. Maybe it was something completely normal, but that I wasn't equipped to detect. Like radon or black mold.

I had a sudden aching longing to talk to Thorbjorn about it. He felt so far away in that moment.

But he was where he needed to be. And so was I.

I just hoped we'd be together again soon.

CHAPTER SEVENTEEN

ᚺ

I WAS STILL SITTING on that front porch, idly paging through my sketchbook while I waited for Esja to come back down the stairs, when the garden gate opened with a bang and Nilda came sprinting up the walk.

She almost ran past me, but pulled up short without quite tripping in the doorway.

"Ingrid!" she said. But that was all she could get out. Her face was sweaty and bright red, and she was completely out of breath.

"Nilda, what's going on?" I asked, stuffing my sketchbook back in my bag and slinging it over my shoulder. I sensed hurry was about to be called for, but there was no way I was sprinting through town in this heat like Nilda had clearly just done. "Did you run all the way here from the caves?"

She nodded, hands on her knees as she caught her breath. Then she swallowed hard and said, "You need to talk to Valki. Now."

"Thorbjorn?" I just managed to choke out.

"No, no, not that," Nilda said, and put a hand on my arm in silent apology. "Nothing's happened. Yet. But Valki is worried something is about to. It's better if he tells you. Can you go to him now?"

"Of course," I said, gripping the strap of my art bag tightly. "Esja just went upstairs to change to go out. Do we need to call that off?"

"No," Nilda said after a moment's thought. "Although Kara and I might have to take her down to the mead hall without you. But hopefully you can catch up later."

"Keep her safe?" I said, even as I started backing towards the still open garden gate.

"We will," Nilda said. She watched from the doorway as I headed out the gate, only turning to go inside at the same instant I latched it shut behind me.

I didn't run, but I did walk as briskly as I could manage. And regretted again not bringing a water bottle with me. It felt like there was more than enough liquid in the air I was laboring to breathe, and yet I could feel myself getting dehydrated all over again as I hustled through the quiet streets of the town.

When I reached the main cavern at the bottom of the stone staircase, Valki was waiting for me in the mouth of the cave that led to the ancestral fire.

"What's going on?" I asked, but he just waved for me to follow him back to the bonfire.

At least there was water there. I filled a cup from the sort of oversized cooler that sports teams used that rested on a wooden table in a shadowed corner of the cavern, drank it down in one gulp, then filled another.

"Nilda told me you went down to see Halldis," Valki said as I drained the second cup and filled it again before joining him at the stools by the flames.

"I did," I said. "Did I need permission?"

"No, obviously not," he said. "I just wished you'd checked in with me, or I could've told you. You weren't the only one down there today."

"What do you mean?" I asked. "Who else could get past her doorway?"

"That is precisely my question," Valki said darkly. "Not the who, I know who. But the how. How did he get past the doorway?"

"Who?" I said. I wanted to know that before I started worrying about the how.

"Roarr," he said.

"Oh." Yeah, that wasn't good news at all. If there was anyone that shouldn't be going down to see Halldis at all, let alone sneaking down without telling anyone, it was Roarr.

But then I tripped on the same question that Valki was tormented by.

How?

"I don't know how he got past me to get down there in the first place," Valki said, staring into the flames as if the answer might be there. "But he did. I didn't notice him until he was leaving again, running out of the caves in a great hurry. But even then I didn't put it together until Nilda was chatting with me about changing the duty rotation for the evening. She mentioned that you had spoken with Halldis, and I suddenly put it together. Where he must have been."

"He can't do magic," I said. "But it's possible he's gotten a hold of another artifact with power."

He had been the one that had found the bronze amulet, the one he gave to Halldis, that had given her access to power that only a trained volva should have had. He hadn't used it for himself, but he hadn't known what it was at the time.

Since then, other artifacts from the wilds outside Villmark had turned up in other people's hands. None of them had been put to good uses.

And we all knew more artifacts still waited to be found, lurking out in the wilds north and west of Villmark.

Places that Roarr passed through when he volunteered for patrol.

"That was my fear," Valki said. "But could such a thing both sneak him past me without my noticing him, and also move the stone for him?"

That didn't seem likely.

But there was always the possibility he had acquired *two* artifacts. Somehow.

I didn't like that thought at all. But it made sense to rule out some less remote possibilities first. There were other ways he could've gotten inside that didn't call for the kind of magic even I couldn't do without the aid of my cat.

"She's been getting deliveries of food and firewood, and I guess water and other things as well," I said.

"Yes, weekly. Whichever of my sons is with me that day, the two of us roll back the stone together. We have two members of the volunteer patrol with us, just in case something should happen while we're occupied with that work. But never Roarr."

"No, obviously not," I said. "He never comes down to the caves at all, does he?"

"He can pass through to Runde, same as anyone, but we do watch his movements more closely than other people's," Valki said. "Which is why it's so worrying that he got past me this once."

"You need more help," I said.

I expected him to argue. For a minute, it looked like he was about to. But then all the anger just left his face. He didn't speak, only gave me a curt nod, but it was enough. I'd bring it up in the next council meeting, and between the two of us, we'd get something done.

Although the idea of having the likes of Raggi and Skefill guarding either the ancestral fire or the prisoners in the cave didn't exactly fill me with reassurance. But there were others in the village that could be trusted. More than just the Thors.

"I think Roarr knows that you are watching him more closely than you watch the others," I said. "He keeps telling me how badly he wants to regain everyone's trust. How hard he's working to do that. And now he's sneaking down to the lower caves? To see her? I don't think he was lying to me before. I think something has changed."

"He's been controlled by her before," Valki said.

"But I just saw her. She's in a very weakened state. I don't see her managing to do anything like that. Even if she could circumvent my grandmother's wards, which I don't think she could even on her best day," I said.

"You saw her after he was down there," Valki said. "Perhaps she expended all of her power bringing him to her."

Maybe. But I didn't think so. She hadn't seemed acutely exhausted. Even then, her glamor would've still clung to her. And then there was the matter of the need for food and fire by conventional means. That wasn't new.

"You saw him leave, but you didn't speak to him?" I asked.

"No. He was gone up the stairs before I had even reached the cavern. Not that I called after him." Then he balled his hands into fists and pressed them to his temples in a rare show of pure frustration. "You are quite right that we need more help down here. I've been deluding myself that I am still at the top of my form, but I am not. I let him slip by me, and then I let him slip away again, even though I saw him. And I was still convincing myself that it hadn't meant anything when Nilda said Halldis's name and I knew I'd been every kind of fool."

"Was it a spell, do you think? From Halldis or from Roarr by means of an artifact of some kind?" I asked.

"No," he said, his face looking more anguished than ever. "No, this is entirely my own doing."

"Someone is coming to relieve you, I hope," I said.

"Thoralv is on his way with one of the volunteers," Valki said. "I was planning to go find Roarr the minute they arrive."

"No, why don't you get some sleep?" I told him. "I can find Roarr. Even if you found him first, I'm still the one who's going to have to ask him all the hard questions. See if he's lying."

"I suppose you are right about that," he said.

"You know, for a fact, he got inside her cell?" I asked.

"Perhaps he only found a way to communicate with her through the stone somehow? In truth, I don't know. All I know is he was down there, and when he left, he left at a full run."

I pondered that. I wanted to say his deduction was based on some pretty shaky assumptions.

Only when I had talked to Halldis, she had seemed to know things. Things I was sure no one bringing her food and firewood would tell her, or even know themselves.

But Roarr had been visiting Esja.

Which, aside from the conundrum of how he'd even gotten down there in the first place, left a second pressing question.

How much had he done willingly, and how much had he been coerced into doing?

Had he really gone down to see Halldis and tell her all about Esja?

Or had he gone down for reasons of his own and let slip a few details she had snatched up greedily to use against me later?

Or had she truly lured him down there, as she had once used magic to lure me into her own home?

"I have to find him right away," I said.

"Yes, go," Valki said. "My son will be here soon, and when he arrives, I'll send word to all the patrols to be on the lookout for Roarr. We've been at a weapons-only level of alert, but perhaps it's time to upgrade to full armor and weapons."

"Not just yet," I said. "Not in this heat."

Valki scoffed at that. "No true Villmarker is undone by a little thing like the weather."

"I know. Just, wait," I said, not quite smiling. Pricking his vanity even that little bit had at least brought him out of his self-recriminating funk, anyway.

I drained one last cup of water, then headed back up to the meadow.

But I had no idea where to start hunting for Roarr. He had gone up the stairs, west towards Villmark, so I guessed that ruled out my grandmother's mead hall.

But Roarr knew other ways out of the barrier that protected Villmark, other ways to get to Runde.

He had used them once to move the body of his dead fiancée to the crossroads on the highway, to shift suspicion away from Halldis. It was really hard to put that thought out of my mind.

I had never quite made up my mind whether I could trust him or not. I wanted to believe he was sincere when he said he wanted to prove himself better than what the others thought of him. But I could never stop myself from thinking it was possible to be both really sincere about your intentions, and completely delusional about your capabilities.

Just because he wanted to be a better person didn't mean he could be.

But I guessed that, one way or another, I was about to find out the real truth about Roarr.

CHAPTER EIGHTEEN

ᚺ

IT WAS STILL afternoon and not yet evening when I emerged back out onto the meadow. The sun was still beating down mercilessly, and the air was too oppressive for me to manage more than a brisk walk. And even then, I could feel the pounding redness of my face before I'd even reached the easternmost edge of town.

I made a beeline through Villmark, out past the western border to Aldís's mead hall.

It just seemed like the most logical place to start my search. It had been fruitful twice before.

But as I pushed open the heavy door and stood blinking in the dark interior, waiting for my sun-dazzled eyes to adjust, I could sense the emptiness of the space around me. There was no crackle of flames, and the smell of cooking meat was clearly only the lingering aromas from the night before.

Or the accumulation of a lot of nights. It had that sort of old grease smell, the smell that was quickly covered by the stronger scents of roasting meat, but emerged again when that meat was gone. Like it clung, not just to the iron grills waiting for the fire pits to be lit once more, but was buried deep in the woodwork all around me.

When my vision finally started picking out details, I saw the place was indeed empty. Save for silver-haired Aldís herself, who was standing in the middle of the room, sizable arms crossed as she waited for me to notice her. She wasn't so much fat as just thick in a way I was more accustomed to seeing in middle-aged men who had been athletes in their young days.

"Torfudottir," she said when she saw I was focusing on her. "Your young friend isn't here."

"No, I can see that," I said. "But I was actually looking for Roarr."

"Roarr Egilsen?" she said with a frown. At my nod, she said, "He's not a regular. I haven't seen him in here in months, and then it was with some of the other young fellows fresh off of patrol. A bit early in the day for that. Can I ask why you're looking for him?"

"If you see him, can you tell him I need to talk to him?" I said. Not remotely answering her question.

But she accepted my response with a good-natured shrug. "Sure. If I see him. But like I said, it's not too likely. But I tell you what, I'll put the word out to my regulars to keep an eye out and pass the message along."

"That would be very helpful, thank you," I said.

In my experience, her regulars were far less likely to want to be helpful to me than she was, but I still appreciated the offer.

I made my way south to Ullr's mead hall. It was just off the public gardens, a short walk from both the council hall and Haraldr's house.

Ullr's mead hall was more like my grandmother's establishment than Aldís's, an airy, open space with stone fireplaces and lots of carved wooden timbers. The long tables were gleamingly clean, the benches turned upside-down to rest on top of them. The flagstone floors must have been mopped the night before, as they were clean now, but also completely dry.

I found Ullr himself in the kitchens, working alone to chop and season a variety of meats in preparation for that evening's dinner customers. He was about a decade older than Aldís, with steel gray hair pulled back as he worked. His roundness was a little more fat than hers, but there wasn't any question to the lingering presence of strong muscle underneath as I watched his arm's tireless motion chopping the meat into cubes ready for skewering.

He wiped his hands on his stained apron and emerged from the kitchen the minute he saw me in the doorway.

"Ingrid Torfudottir. It's been too long. But I guess you're not here now for dinner and a drink?" he said.

"Alas, no. I'm looking for Roarr," I said.

"Ah, Roarr," he said, nodding. "He was here last night, for a spell. But I've not quite opened for business yet today. Are you investigating something? I don't recall who he was with or when he left, but I'm sure one of my servers would remember something. They'll be trickling in any minute now."

"No, he didn't do anything last night," I said. Which, so far as I knew, was true. "I just need to speak with him. If he does come in, can you let him know I'm looking for him?"

"Certainly," he said. "I hope it's nothing serious?"

He was clearly gently probing for more details, but all I said was, "Me, too."

Then I was back outside, fast-walking to the closest of the other mead halls.

By the time I was checking the last of the mead halls in town, the sun was setting and the smells from the meat they were all cooking now had my stomach growling. But I didn't dare stop to sample anything.

Although when one of the mead hall owners shoved half a loaf of freshly baked brown bread into my hands, then added a wedge of dark orange cheese, I didn't say no.

I stood at the edge of the marketplace, watching the shops close up for the night, as I pondered my options.

Everyone had promised to spread the word, and I knew they had because half the people passing me on the street paused a moment to let me know that they hadn't seen Roarr, but they were on the lookout.

Which was helpful. But also maddening. Because at this point, it was starting to feel like he wasn't even in Villmark.

Valki would've gotten word to all the patrols by now. But the patrols couldn't be the tightest of nets. If Roarr had any suspicion that he was being looked for, it would be all too easy for him to evade those patrols.

He could be anywhere.

But there were still places in town I hadn't checked yet.

Which was why, as I chewed the last of the bread and cheese, I left the marketplace and headed south again.

To Halldis's cottage.

It had been a cool September night when she had lured me there before.

No, not lured. She had controlled me like a puppet. She had walked me straight into her home. Into her greatest place of power.

It was still light out now, the setting sun lighting up the windows around me in splashes of red and orange. And the lingering heat in the air was another reminder that this time was different. I was walking that path of my own free will.

But even so, when I reached the beginning of the alley that led to her tucked-away cottage, I stopped to take out my wand again.

I wished Mjolner was there with me. But I knew if I truly needed him, he'd be there already. He always was.

And by the same token, if he wasn't here, he knew I was okay. I didn't need him.

I could do this on my own.

I walked through the break in the garden fences between two houses, down the narrow alley, towards the glimpse of red I could just see up ahead. The red front door of her cottage.

My grandmother had pulled out everything in Halldis's herb garden the autumn before. I wouldn't be surprised if she had come back in the spring and summer, just to be sure. Most of what Halldis had been growing had been completely benign, the usual culinary and medicinal herbs, the kinds of things you didn't need to be a volva to use.

But she had been growing other things as well. And my grandmother wasn't taking any chances.

There was green all around me as I emerged from between the two fences, but it was all weeds. Mostly of the noxious, stinging variety. Nothing so lovely as a thistle or a dandelion anywhere.

But that just made sense. The whole place felt noxious. Unwholesome. Nothing beautiful or good would thrive here. But bad things could.

I pushed that thought aside, trying not to brush up against any of the weeds as I made my way to the door and pushed it open.

The interior of her cottage was much as I had remembered it. The roof was quite gone now, the center burned out, but the remaining thatch around the edges at the walls was starting to gray and crumble away as well.

No herbs hung from the rafters, and the rafters themselves were scarred from smoke and here and there actually blackened from fire damage.

The furniture was all gone as well. It made the space feel larger than I remembered. It also felt empty, not just physically but also magically.

Halldis not being here had left a palpable void. I wasn't sure if anyone else would feel it the way I did. My grandmother, perhaps.

But I don't think she had ever felt as overwhelmed by the presence of Halldis as I had that night, trapped here, at her mercy.

I took a deep breath, then pushed those memories back to the darker corners of my mind.

Then I looked at the floor. There were scattered dried leaves and bits of straw that had fallen from the damaged thatching above. But they were just decorative touches over the base, a thick layer of dust that coated all the floorboards.

Some mice had crossed that space at some point in the recent past, but nothing else. Certainly not Roarr.

If he had gotten a hold of a magical artifact, he hadn't gotten it from here. Which was heartening in a way. It meant my grandmother hadn't missed anything when she'd cleared the place out.

But it increased the odds that Roarr had found whatever he had found outside of the town.

And it just followed that if he had, then he was likely outside of the town now too.

I really only had one place left to check.

I arrived at his parents' house just as the last sliver of sun was sliding down behind the hills to the west. I could see where it had just been, lighting up the trees and turning their green tops to a golden hue. A beautiful sunset, one meant to be enjoyed from a comfortable chair, beverage in hand, with the smell of grilling food almost ready to be consumed.

At least the bread and cheese I had eaten before had been filling. All I really longed for now was a rest off my feet, and the peace of mind of all being well in Villmark.

But I wasn't there yet.

I knocked on the door. It was opened almost at once by Roarr's father Egil and his mother Ragna.

I could tell by the worried sadness in their eyes that they both knew I was looking for Roarr, and that they didn't know where he was.

It was like I could feel myself deflating, there on their doorstep.

"He left about midmorning," Egil said. His voice was thick, like the words themselves were strangling him.

"We don't know where he's gone," Ragna said.

"But I looked in his room just now. His bedroll and camping gear are gone," Egil said.

I nodded. I really didn't want to grill them any harder. They'd already been through so much, back when the entire village had thought their son a murder. And then again, when he had been a suspect in yet another murder.

It had been a tough year for them.

But I still had to ask. "How did he seem when you saw him this morning? Was he his usual self? Or like... before," I finished lamely.

But they both knew what I meant.

"I didn't really talk with him myself," Egil said. "I was on my way out just as he came down the stairs. We traded good morning nods. He seemed fine."

He looked down at his wife. She had a handkerchief in her hand, wadded and twisted already, and she was fidgeting with it now. But her eyes were dry. She was distraught, but tear-free.

"He seemed fine," she said at last. "Not like before. But like he's been ever since."

So, not exactly *fine*, but we were grading Roarr on a curve here.

"And he didn't have his gear with him when he left?" I asked.

"No, not in the morning. But we were both out for most of the day. He must've come back at some point and gotten it," she said.

"Or he had cached it somewhere earlier than this morning," Egil said.

"Has he been using it on patrol or anything?" I asked.

"No, he patrols close to town. No overnights," Egil said.

"Sometimes he's out at night, but he's never gone for more than twelve hours at a time. He sleeps in his own bed," Ragna said.

"Okay, thanks," I said, trying not to sound as tired as I felt. "When I find him, I'll tell him to check in with both of you. He shouldn't be making you worry like this."

"He's been doing so well lately," Ragna said. "Working on the patrols, hanging out with friends. He was getting so close to his old self. I had really hoped—"

She broke off, not quite with a sob, but as if she didn't want to keep talking lest a sob actually did take over her.

"I don't know that anything is wrong, exactly," I said. "It's still possible that this is all a misunderstanding."

"But you went to see Halldis," Egil said.

So that word had gotten around as well.

They were both looking the same question at me. And I really wished I could answer it.

But I couldn't. I didn't know for a fact that she wasn't somehow manipulating their son again.

"I'm going to find him," was all I could promise them.

Then I left at a jog, determined to do just that.

CHAPTER NINETEEN

ᚺ

I HAD JUST REACHED the village commons on my way back to the Mikkelsens' house when I saw the Mikkelsen sisters heading my way.

My heart sank before they even got close enough for me to see the worry and alarm on their faces.

Esja wasn't with them. And they wouldn't be looking this upset if they hadn't already gone to Aldís's mead hall and failed to find her there.

"How long?" I asked as they skidded to a stop in front of me.

"She was in her room when I went upstairs," Nilda said. "I saw her. I talked to her. She was dressed and ready to go, but she wanted to wait in case you came back in time to go out with us. I didn't object. I wanted a shower before we went out, anyway."

"Of course," I said. She was dressed in a different outfit than when I had seen her last, but if she had gotten that shower, all the running she'd done since then had undone its effects.

Not that I was going to point that out.

"I left Esja in her room and went to talk to Kara. I don't know when she left, but it was after that."

"We went to tell her it was time to go without you, and she was gone," Kara said. "There was maybe half an hour when we weren't watching her. If that."

"I sealed her window," I said. "With magic."

"Her windows were still closed. I guess she walked right out the front door this time," Nilda said.

"For all the good that did us," Kara grumbled.

"What was she wearing? The same kind of thing as before?" I asked.

"No, actually," Nilda said. "She had modern clothes. I don't know where she got them—"

"Sigvin," Kara put in.

Nilda just shrugged. "She was wearing jeans and a sleeveless blouse. It was white with white embroidery around the neckline. It was really nice."

"She took a sweatshirt with her, too," Kara said. "She had this hoodie from the football team Vikings. She liked to wear it around the house in the evenings when it was chilly. So not lately."

"Yeah, but it was draped over the back of her chair when I was talking to her, and when she left, she took it with her," Nilda said.

"Can you tell if she packed a bag?" I asked.

They looked at each other with real horror.

"You think she's run away for good? That she's not coming back?" Nilda asked me.

"I think she might have left with Roarr, and Roarr took camping gear with him," I said. "What about her shoes? Practical for dancing or something else?"

"She seems to prefer barefoot for dancing," Kara said wryly.

"Hiking shoes," Nilda said. "New, like the jeans."

I chewed at my lip. Yeah, it was starting to sound like she and Roarr had run away together. Why else would a housebound young woman wear hiking shoes when she's planning to go out dancing?

"You've been all over Villmark already, or so it seemed when we were looking for you," Nilda said. "What do you want us to do now? Go with you out of town?"

"Not just yet," I said. "I have to go home to pack some things first.

And maybe try to work out which direction they might have gone, because honestly, I don't have a clue. Especially if no one has seen them. Which, at least, I'm pretty confident Valki was the last person to see Roarr, and he only knew Roarr had headed towards town."

"We'll pack too," Kara said.

But I was already shaking my head. "No, stay here in case I'm wrong and they've never left, or if I'm right, but they come back home on their own before I find them."

"We can be more help than that," Nilda said.

"Yes, but you also have responsibilities here in town. Honestly, Valki is exhausted. Until we get more help, I can't take away what little of it he has that he can rely on."

They exchanged a look, but gave in with reluctant nods.

"But check Esja's room. See if she packed a bag. And what she packed. I'm curious if she took her paints with her, or everything she owns, or just an overnight bag," I said.

"Sure, we can do that," Kara said. "You'll be at your house in town, or at the cabin?"

My cabin. I longed for my cabin.

But I had to say, "My house in town. Most of my stuff is still there. I'll have to do some kind of magic before I go, just to get a clue which direction to start looking. I don't fancy wandering around all night in this heat hoping to get lucky."

"The patrols are looking. Be sure to tell us which way you're going, just in case. If anyone sees anything, we'll try to catch up and send you in the right direction," Nilda said.

"Thanks," I said.

But Kara was watching me closely, studying my face.

"There's something more," she guessed. Correctly.

I sighed. "I promised Esja I wouldn't try to get a message to Loke. She didn't want to distract him from whatever it is that he's doing. But I can't keep that promise now."

"Of course not," Kara said. "He would want to know."

"I know," I said.

But it didn't feel any less like betraying a trust.

We parted ways, and I walked the rest of the way to my own garden gate.

Mjolner was waiting for me the minute I opened the front door. As if he'd been sitting primly in my front hall for hours.

"You always know when I need you," I said to him as I went into my living room and dumped my art bag on the chair in front of my worktable and easels. I would need to pack fresh charcoal pencils and a spare sketchbook, for sure.

And water. I wasn't leaving the house again without as much water as I could carry.

Mjolner followed me up to my bedroom, sitting in the doorway and watching me move from my dresser to the open bag at the foot of my bed. He slow-blinked at me, but didn't interrupt.

I hoped it wouldn't take long to catch up with Roarr and Esja. He could make good time on a hike, I was sure. But her I had less of an idea about.

She was stronger than she had ever been before.

But she had never walked for more than twenty minutes at a time. And even then, in my experience, she took lots of rest breaks.

She could probably keep going without rest now that her stamina was increased, but there was more to hiking than stamina.

Things like blisters or sprains from walking on uneven ground when you weren't used to it were possibilities.

But not ones I wanted to count on. I added a few more changes of underwear and socks to the bag before closing it up.

If I packed any more, the weight would be an issue. And I still needed to add food and clean water to the side pouches.

Mjolner blinked at me again as I stood in the middle of the room, dithering about what to do next.

But it was an expectant sort of blink. Like he was reminding me that he was awaiting orders.

I stopped and looked at him, and he blinked at me again. Slow and calming.

"I need you to find Thorbjorn," I said to him at last.

He tipped his head slightly to one side, then tipped it level again.

"No, not Loke. Thorbjorn. He will have a better understanding of Loke's situation than we do. He can make the decision on whether Loke should be told about Esja or not," I said.

Mjolner considered this, then made the softest of mews.

"I'm taking that as agreement," I said.

He flicked one of his ears as if he felt a tickle and wanted to make sure it wasn't a fly or a mosquito.

But he didn't leave. Which was a little odd. Normally, when I asked him to do something, he tore off to do it at once. With an uncatlike sense of obligated hurry.

"What is it?" I asked him.

He just blinked at me again. Patiently.

"Do *you* know which way Roarr and Esja went?" I asked him.

Not that I had any idea how he was supposed to convey this information to me if the answer even was yes. I felt a little foolish even asking him out loud. It was like I was trying to dodge work myself, expecting my cat to do it for me.

Lazy, but also a little deluded.

And yet when Mjolner got up and started walking away down the corridor, I followed behind him. His gait was unhurried, his tail flicking in a syncopated rhythm to his own steps. He took the stairs at something closer to a run, then sauntered into the living room.

And disappeared into my art nook.

I ran back to grab the bag from the bed then went downstairs.

Mjolner was still in the art nook, using one six-toed paw to pull portfolio after portfolio down from my neatly arranged bookshelf filled with my sketchbooks and other work.

"Can I help you find something?" I asked, fighting what I think is pretty understandable frustration. He was making such a mess.

He meowed in a way that I took to mean yes. So I set my backpack next to my art bag, then started pulling down portfolios one by one. But more neatly than he had done it.

I showed him the covers of each, carefully labeled with the range of dates of the work contained within, but he looked away with disinterest from all of them.

Then I pulled out my sketchbooks. These were also arranged by date, but in this case they were written on the inside of the front cover, so I had to open each to show him.

I was starting to think he was messing with me, when I finally found one that he didn't turn away from. In fact, he lunged forward to paw at it, like he wanted to turn the pages himself.

I set it down on the floor and turned the pages one by one until he put his paw down firmly on top of the book.

On a sketch I had drawn of Loke with a pair of knives facing down against an enormous white wolf. A white wolf that had magically fallen from the sky.

"There?" I said. That had been in the middle of a forest. A forest I had gotten to after Loke had done his teleportation trick, jumping from the front door of this very house to the burned-out remains of a doorway in an abandoned village.

A village that had been centered around a well. The well marked the location where the wolf had landed after falling out of the clear blue sky, hitting the earth and starting its hunt.

Loke and another Villmarker named Báfurr had slain it.

But that hadn't been the end of things that were connected to this nameless abandoned village. I knew the strange women who looked like ageless sisters, women like Halldis, had all come from that village.

And I suspected some of their power, which was a different sort of magic than the kind volvas used, was centered around that well.

"Roarr went here," I said to Mjolner, just to clarify. I turned back a few pages in the book. I had drawn this village in a magical fugue state before I'd ever seen it with my own eyes. It was north and west of Villmark.

But I had never walked the ground between. Nilda had, when she had gone in search of those strange women months ago. She had found nothing.

But thanks to her telling me about her journey, I had an idea of where it might be. If only a vague one.

Mjolner meowed at me again, chidingly.

"Are you trying to tell me that of course I can find it?" I asked him. "Because I'm not sure that's true."

He meowed again, then slapped his paw in the center of the sketch I had turned the page to. Right on top of that well.

"Oh, sure," I said. "A magic well. I can probably find that. I mean, I'll sense its direction, anyway."

And I knew the whole village was on a road. A road that had fallen into disuse centuries ago, but a road all the same.

Mjolner meowed again, but in a self-satisfied kind of way.

"When you see Thorbjorn, tell him I miss him," I said.

He rubbed the top of his head against the side of my thigh.

But then he jumped up and sprinted down the hallway faster than a kitten with the zoomies. I crawled to the edge of the living room to see the front door just as closed as I had left it. But there was no sign of Mjolner.

He was off on his mission.

It was time for me to head out on mine.

CHAPTER TWENTY

ᚺ

THE IDEA of walking the entire way to that village was daunting. I knew it would take more than a day to get there, and I was starting at sunset when I was already exhausted from a day of running around in the heat.

So when I stepped out of my front gate, two heavy bags over my shoulder and my sturdiest walking stick in my hand, I was at once relieved to see Kara there waiting for me.

Well, not so much Kara as the wagon that was parked behind her.

"You'll be faster driving than walking," she said as she stroked the head of the horse who was yoked up to the wagon. "You remember how to take care of this fella?"

"Yes," I said. "Thanks. I know where I'm going now, but it's not exactly close. And I don't know what I'm going to find when I get there."

"Esja packed a bag," Kara told me as she helped me set my bags in the back of the wagon. "All her socks and underwear are gone, but she left her dresses and skirts behind. Nilda guesses she acquired more than just the one pair of jeans."

"It sounds that way to me," I agreed.

"Is she going north?" Kara asked, lowering her voice as if wary of being overheard. But there was no one on the street but the two of us, not for at least a block, and that party of walkers was heading south to Ullr's mead hall.

"Not directly," I said. "Not to the tower where the Thors were held, anyway."

"That is indeed what I was afraid of," Kara said. "Although some random village doesn't exactly fill my heart with joy, either."

"I don't think it's random. In fact, it's the village where Nilda went looking for Hulda, after we all got back from the north. She found nothing, so I don't know why Esja is heading that way."

"I don't like the sound of it," Kara said.

"Nor I. But I'll know more when I get there," I said. She watched me climb up into the wagon's seat and take up the reins.

I had driven this wagon a few times before. As nervous as I was to get started, I knew it would come back to me soon enough.

And the idea of stopping for the night with a bed all ready and waiting for me within the walls of the wagon that the three of us—my grandmother, Kara and I—had already protected with bind runes and wards was so much better than what I had been expecting to have to do.

Which was stop at the side of the road and try to find the friend-liest-looking tree. I hadn't even packed a blanket, let alone a sleeping bag.

"I can still come with you," Kara said.

"No, you're needed here," I said. But then I added, "I sent Mjolner to find Thorbjorn."

"To come back home?" Kara asked.

"Well, no. To determine if anything should be told to Loke or not. But I guess I am kind of hoping he comes back to help me," I admitted.

"If he can, I'm sure he will," Kara said with total confidence.

More confidence than I felt, anyway. But I smiled at her, then got the horse moving.

I knew I couldn't keep driving all night long. Even with the moon at its fullest high above, the old road would get too dark further into the forest.

But I kept going for as long as I could, for as long as the horse could see to keep stepping forward and as long as I could remain sitting upright in the driver's seat.

I made it past midnight. But just barely.

I unhitched the horse, rubbed it down and got it fed and watered, then sat on the back step of the wagon to have my own dinner of pastries and bread rolls I had grabbed from the assortment of thank you baskets from the farmers that someone from the council had piled up in my kitchen while I was out.

I had never quite gotten around to grocery shopping since the hailstorm had driven me back into town. But the farmers had been generous in their thanks. More carbs than protein, but I really didn't mind.

I double-checked all the wards on the wagon before I went inside, but all the spells were holding strong.

Kara and Thorge hadn't changed a thing about the wagon's interior. But my grandmother's friend Reginleif had kept it tastefully decorated, so I could see why they'd left it as it was.

The little table on my left with its long blue cloth always reminded me of a fortuneteller's table, and the two little stools that were arranged around it were impossible for a Thor to use. But somehow Thorge had managed, as they were still there, and intact.

The kitchen on the right was neatly arranged, plates, pots and pans stowed in the closed cabinets, the bucket that functioned as a sink chained in place below them but currently empty.

But what really called to me was the bed at the far side of the wagon. There wasn't much headroom to sit up on it. Every bit of space that could be used for storage had been, so there was yet another row of cabinets over the bed. I had to fold over and slide into it sideways.

The only thing that was lacking to make this place entirely homey was my cat, Mjolner, sleeping on the pillow.

But I was going to have to sleep without him for the next few days.

I got into that neatly made bed. For the first minute or so, I desperately missed the warmth of my cat against the back of my neck.

Then I fell into deep and dreamless sleep.

When I woke, the sun had not yet risen. Everything was gray and a little hazy, the humidity in the guise of something like fog as it waited for the sun to heat it up properly.

I hitched up the horse and got going before digging out more bread rolls and pastries for breakfast.

I admit I dozed off and on as the horse carried the wagon and me along. But the almost liquid warmth of the air and the quiet of the woods around the road conspired to make me extra sleepy.

That, plus so many nights of not enough sleep to deal with my accumulated exhaustion. I hadn't caught up on needed rest since the hailstorm had turned my life upside down.

But a stiff breeze picked up in the afternoon, almost chilly as it sliced through the humid air and chased it away. Clouds came scuttling across the sky. Not storm clouds, nothing so large and dark as that. But their puffy forms were growing darker and more sprawled out as the day progressed.

I took to not just scanning the road ahead of us for signs of threats in the woods on either side, but also for any hint of the magic I knew would be associated with that well. I knew I was heading in the right direction, but the further along I went, the more just heading northwest wasn't going to be accurate enough to get me there.

I could sense something up ahead of me. Something like a thrum at the back of my mind. But I didn't see anything. Not even in my magical vision.

But it functioned as a beacon for me all the same. I knew I was heading the right way, so long as that thrum felt like its source was still ahead of me.

I reached the outskirts of that village by midafternoon. I recognized it at once, both from my sketch and from the day I had spent here with Loke, searching for Báfurr.

The homes were like Aldís's mead hall, built from stone walls with the remains of sod roofs still standing on a few of them. But most were roofless now, and the stones of the walls were starting to tumble down. The timber of the doorframes was crumbling away.

The sound of the wagon wheels on the road and of the horse's hooves echoed eerily. The homes were clustered at a crossroads, but were still widely spaced. Unlike Villmark, the gardens around these places had been necessary for food production. They took up a lot of space because of that. And there were no wooden privacy fences anywhere. Just low stone walls that marked the boundaries, not tall enough to keep anyone out. Not even a rabbit.

Basically, there was nothing about this place that should be causing an echo.

I was still puzzling about that when the well at the center of the crossroads itself finally came into view.

And so did Roarr. And Esja.

He was grabbing at her arm, trying to pull her away with him. And she was twisting, trying to free herself.

I was off the driver's seat in a flash, leaving the horse and wagon standing in the middle of the road as I charged forward. I had my wand with me, already in my hand.

"Roarr! Stop!" I shouted.

He let go of Esja at once, spinning around to face me.

I raised my wand, expecting him to charge me. But he didn't.

No, the look on his face was one of complete relief.

"Ingrid! Thank the gods! I've been trying to get her to come home, but she won't listen to me," he said.

I looked from him to Esja. The instant he had released her, she had moved away from him. She was striding up to the well now, hands at her sides but flexing open and closed, open and closed.

"What's going on here?" I asked.

"I followed her here so I could stop her. She doesn't know what she's doing. She doesn't know what this place is," Roarr said. "Ingrid, we have to stop her."

"Stop her from doing what?" I asked.

As if on cue, Esja started dancing. I noticed then she had taken her hiking shoes off. They were waiting for her at the edge of the grassy circle at the heart of the crossroads, together with her mud-spattered socks and her overnight bag.

Now she was dancing barefoot over the grass, spinning and spinning as she circled the well.

But this wasn't like when I had seen her dancing in the mead hall. Because I could see the magic roiling through her. It was like a storm of power raging inside her tiny body.

It was inside of her, but it wasn't *of* her. It wasn't her magic. It was some alien, invading thing.

I knew now what had made Kara so sick when she had caught a glimpse of it before. I knew better how to shield myself from its effects, but still. It was hard to look at.

And yet, I didn't dare look away. Even when the aching pressure started to set in behind my eyes.

This was the source of the thrum I had been following. My beacon had been Esja, not the well.

And yet, the well was why she was here. I knew that. I just didn't know why.

"That well is a bad place," Roarr whispered to me.

"I know that," I said. "But what is she *doing*?"

But I knew what she was doing. I could see it happening. As she danced, her arms spiraling up and down like a figure skater's, I could see the magic weaving around her.

She wasn't creating it. She didn't have that power.

But she didn't need to. She was drawing something I couldn't see, not even with my strongest magic-detecting senses, something from deep down within that well. She was drawing it up, and as it swirled around her dancing form, it took on the distinctive glow of magic. Magic as I was used to seeing it, albeit in its rawest form.

And her dance was working it. Spinning it into a golden thread of power. And weaving that thread into a spell pattern.

But what spell was she weaving?

"Esja," I said, leaving Roarr standing there to advance on her. I tried to catch her arm, but she evaded me without even losing her place in her dance. It was like she was an eel in water, she just slipped through my fingers.

"This is the exact village that Halldis came from," Roarr said, his voice getting almost shrill, like he was on the edge of panic. "She could never tap the power here herself, it was forbidden to her. I don't know why. But now Esja has been called here. But she's not after anything so small as the power that Halldis had, through that amulet. She's after everything. All the power."

"You didn't think to tell me this *before* you came running after her?" I spun to say to him. "We could've come out here together. Faster, if I'd known what was going on."

"I wanted to—" he started to say. But he was looking past me. He gave up trying to explain himself with a huff of frustration, then ran at Esja again, trying to tackle her to the ground.

Her dance added another little spin, taking her just out of his reach before spiraling in towards the well again.

She was humming something without words. It was no tune I had ever heard before, but still. It felt like it ought to be familiar. A memory of a memory.

"We have to stop her," Roarr said. "I've been trying to grab her since I got here. I almost had her a second ago."

Except I had interrupted him. Although he didn't say that.

"Right," I said, and lowered my wand. I didn't know what spell she was weaving, but I didn't need to know. I could just disrupt it. Pull the threads of it apart and watch the pattern unravel.

Then Roarr and I together could figure out a way to keep her from starting it all over again. Because I was sure she was going to want to.

And she had more strength than Nilda and Kara together when she needed it. When someone tried to stop her doing what she wanted to do.

Or, not *her*. Whatever was working through her. The dark power her body could barely contain.

Esja danced by me again, the woven magic trailing from her gesturing hands, flowing like the ribbon of a gymnast doing a floor routine.

I lunged forward. She evaded me within her dance again, but that was just fine.

She hadn't been my target, anyway.

I jabbed my wand just where she had been, catching both of the ribbons of spell that fluttered behind her hands. I looped my wand around a few times, like I was doing the world's craziest crochet stitch yarn-over.

And then I pulled.

Esja shrieked in rage. Or rather, whatever was inside her did. The sound came from her mouth, which gaped open, but it definitely wasn't her voice.

It sounded like it came from some monstrous thing, some dragon or wyrm or forgotten creature from older times.

Then, to my shock and surprise, she pulled back. She yanked her woven spell free of my grasp with such force not only did I not manage to hold on to it, I was pulled off my feet to face-plant into the grass.

I had just barely missed catching my forehead on the edge of the stone-walled well.

Roarr ran up to help me back to my feet, and the two of us stumbled back as Esja danced by us once more.

"She came out here on her own to do this?" I asked.

"Depends on what you mean by on her own," Roarr said, dabbing at his nose with the back of his hand. There was dried blood in both places. Apparently, he'd already learned the hard way what Esja could do now.

"*You* didn't bring her here after you spoke with Halldis," I said.

"What? No! I told you, I ran after her to stop her. I just couldn't catch up to her in time," he said. "She never stopped. All night long, she kept moving. It was all I could do to stay on her trail and not fall too far behind."

"So you know what she's doing?" I asked.

"Not really," he admitted. "But if Halldis was gloating about it, I knew it had to be bad. Ingrid, we have to stop her. Can't you try something else?"

I bit at my lip. How much power did I want to unleash here? Because as much as Esja's spellwork was giving her something like super strength, underneath all that, it was still Esja. No longer so frail, but still so tiny.

"Ingrid," Roarr said again, desperately.

"Right," I said grimly, and lowered my wand.

But whatever I was about to do, I never even got a chance to try. Because in that instant Esja started spinning with unnatural speed, and all those spells wrapped in tight around her.

Then she stopped dancing, bending at the waist and throwing her arms forward in a whip-like motion.

Sending all the magic she had pulled up—and given order to its chaos, weaving the threads together into an intricate spell whose purpose I still didn't know—back down into that well.

And then the world exploded.

CHAPTER TWENTY-ONE

ᚺ

I WAS on the ground again. That much I knew for sure.

But my vision was nothing but exploding black stars, like photo-negative fireworks, growing and overlapping, then bursting anew.

My ears were ringing, but distantly. Like I could hear something on a pool deck ringing, but only through so much water because I was sitting on the bottom of the deep end.

And I had a weird electric taste in my mouth. It was like the smell of burned circuits was lingering on my tongue, strange and gross.

Something was touching me, like a hand on my shoulder. Then it moved away from me, darting away with a rustle that just reached me through the watery ringing.

Roarr. Roarr had recovered faster than I had. And he was trying to tackle Esja again.

What had she done?

I blinked hard as my vision started to clear. I was looking down at the grassy earth between my hands as I crouched on hands and knees.

There was blood dripping down, staining the blades of grass between my hands. I had a nosebleed.

I ignored that, looking up instead. I saw Roarr stumbling his way towards Esja.

Esja, who was dancing again, but this time on the very top of the stone wall that circled the well. She was spinning drunkenly about, always looking like she was about to fall down into the well, but then recovering with some improbable step that let her catch herself just in time.

She looked like she was on fire. But the flames licking around her limbs were flames of magic. They didn't seem to be consuming her, but it was still hard to look at. So bright.

So wrong.

But she was also saying something. I could see her mouth moving, but the ringing in my ears had shifted into a roar. I sat back on my heels, pressing the palms of my hands over my ears like that would somehow help.

Then all at once her voice reached me clearly. Only, like with the shrieking before, it wasn't really her voice.

And I had no idea what language she was speaking. Since coming to Villmark, I had learned modern Villmarker Norse and had developed an ear for some of the older variants of Norse. More in written form than spoken, sure, but still.

The words coming out of her mouth were none of those.

Then she started laughing, lifting her arms up as a pillar of glowing power fired up out of the well to pierce the sky.

I had seen something like this before, when my grandmother had overdone the spells that protected her mead hall. It had been like a beacon, and we had all struggled to contain it before it lured other beings, beings who fed on such power, to us.

We had succeeded then. All of us working together, we'd barely succeeded.

But it was just me now.

And these spells were nothing like the spells my grandmother had cast around her mead hall. These spells I wasn't familiar with at all.

I could see the weave of them as they rushed past me, stabbing up into the sky. But the threads that made up their patterns were a mystery to me, and the patterns of their weaving were an order so complex it seemed to loop back around to chaos again.

I looked down at the ground and saw my wand lying there. I picked it up, struggled to my feet, and raised it high.

Esja spun in another crazy, drunken lurch, stopping herself with a touch of one bare foot so that she ended facing me. Watching me summoning up power of my own.

This time, when she laughed, she was laughing right at me.

I jabbed at her with my wand, although I was too far away to catch any of the magic streaming up past her.

But that hadn't been my goal. Because while she was laughing at me, she wasn't looking at Roarr.

Who had crept up behind her, finally close enough to tackle her.

She shrieked as she felt his arms close around her, but she couldn't fight him off.

He lifted her up off the wall of the well and stumbled backwards as her feet kicked at the air.

Once he had her clear, I dropped my wand and rushed forward.

I didn't know what magic I could use to stop anything. Not with my wand.

But I could think of some more brute force methods like Roarr had just deployed.

I rushed to the edge of the well, put my shoulder against the crumbled remains of the stone wall that circled it, and pushed with all my might.

These stones had stood for centuries. As much as they'd looked like they'd been ready to tumble down even as Esja danced on them, it was harder than I thought to actually get them moving. I could already sense how sore my muscles were going to be in the morning.

But the very difficulty of the task told me my hunch had been correct. These stones were more than a mere way of marking the hole, to keep children or animals from falling down into it.

They had been placed there to serve a magical function. I didn't sense them the way I sensed my grandmother's wards, and I didn't see a single rune carved on any of them. But they still felt like guardian objects.

I pushed with all my might, physical and magical both. And I succeeded. The stones started to fall.

Esja shrieked and shrieked as the stones fell into the open mouth of the well. I circled around to do the same again, just to my right where the wall was still standing. Then again and again until I had pushed all four quadrants down into the well.

And the chaotic, dark power from below was blocked off.

The pillar flickered and faded from the sky, although the hole it had burned through the clouds above took longer to close up.

And Esja's screams shifted from the bone-chilling shrieks of an ancient monster to the shredded remains of her own human voice.

Then she was sobbing. And Roarr was saying something to her close to her ear, too low for me to hear.

But that was all right. She was calming down, whatever he was telling her.

And I was nearly too exhausted to move.

But not moving wasn't an option. In fact, getting away from this place as quickly as possible was imperative.

The beacon was gone, but it had been seen. Probably all the way to the mountains of Old Norway in the north. Or to the wilds west of the tree-covered hills.

Things would be coming. Bad things.

So as much as I wanted to close my eyes and slip into sleep, instead I pushed myself to my feet. I went back to retrieve my wand, tucking it into my pocket.

Then I went back for one last look at the remains of the well. I stood at the very edge of the grassy ring that now was its only border, and looked down.

I couldn't see the watery bottom. I couldn't even see its newly formed bottom of fallen stones. It was too far down, even for the afternoon sun to reach it.

Which I didn't like at all. I wanted to see those stones choking whatever it was off. I wanted to see and be sure. Would they continue to serve as guardians against what lurked below? The power I couldn't see or sense at all?

But it wasn't possible for me to know.

"How did you know that would work?" Roarr asked me. Esja was quiet in his arms now, snuffling against the collar of his shirt. Her arms were dangling awkwardly between her own legs, her hands hanging uselessly from her wrists. She was like a doll that had been thrown aggressively hard into the ground. Not quite broken, but definitely scatter-limbed.

How had I known it would work? I hadn't. I hadn't known at all. I'd only had a momentary hunch. The spells had reminded me of my grandmother's mead hall. That was all I had known to act on.

"Walls contain things," I said, kicking one last little pebble into the well. "If the power is confined to a space like this, the walls probably serve a containing function."

"So you plugged the hole," he said. He sounded relieved, like he was letting his panic go.

But I was afraid it might be a little early for that reaction.

"I'm not saying this is a permanent solution," I said. "I need to talk to my grandmother about this."

"Where am I?" Esja asked in a small, shaky voice. She pushed the hair back from her face and looked around at the remains of the abandoned village, then at me, and then at Roarr.

"We followed you here," Roarr told her. "Don't you know why you came here?"

"I don't even know where here is. I just wanted to get out of the house," she said. "I wanted to go for a walk."

Then she looked up at Roarr like she wanted to say something more. And he looked back at her, eager to hear it.

But then she slumped in his arms as if she'd fallen into a dead faint.

"Esja?" he said, shaking her gently. Then he called her name again and shook her a little harder.

"Is she breathing?" I asked him.

He leaned closer to her face, then looked up at me with a nod.

"Then she'll be all right. I brought a wagon. Let's get her into it and bring her back to town," I said.

Roarr nodded again.

I scanned the horizon around the village, but there was no sign of Thorbjorn, or Mjolner, or Loke.

But I really didn't think it was wise to linger. It would be getting dark soon. And that pillar of raw power would be drawing things to the remains of this village. I had no doubt about that.

And there I was, without a single Thor to fight those things away.

Nothing to do but run back to town. And hope that when Esja woke up again, she could tell me something, anything, about what had just happened here.

But I didn't think her lack of memory of the last day was a ruse. And I doubted a good night's sleep would be enough to bring anything back to her.

The thing hiding within her had hidden well. It might even still be in there, somewhere.

Esja wouldn't be able to tell me. I didn't think she could even sense it within her at all.

I would have to find another way to answer all my questions.

CHAPTER TWENTY-TWO

ᚺ

Roarr had more experience with horses than I did, so when he took the reins without asking, I didn't object. He got us rolling back towards home at a steady pace the horse could manage.

And I took what little opportunity I still had to draw everything.

I drew what I could see of the well and the village until the wagon I was sitting on the back of rolled too far away for me to see any of the details anymore.

Then I drew everything I remembered happening while the memories were still fresh.

Some of them were fading already. I felt like I had gotten some sense of what it was that Esja had been drawing up out of the well, but when I taxed my mind now, I couldn't come up with a single image. Not even a vague sensation.

She had been pulling something up, some force of great, but raw, power.

And yet I couldn't describe it in any way. It was like my mind just skipped over it. I could only see the emptiness where its characteristics should be.

The sun set, taking its light with it, and I shut my book. I had nothing more to draw, anyway.

I crawled back to the front of the wagon.

"We'll have to camp soon," Roarr said to me as I climbed onto the seat beside him. "The horse can't keep going all night."

"No, of course," I said. "I want to check on Esja, anyway."

"I'm glad you came with a wagon," he said. "I don't suppose it's much protection against the things that lurk out in these woods, but it's something."

"It's a protected space," I told him. "Mormor and I put wards on it to keep Kara and Thorge safe. It will do the same for us."

He nodded. As much as he didn't show it, I could feel his weariness as I sat next to him. If he'd been running after Esja all night long, only catching her minutes before I showed up, I could well imagine how tired he must be.

And yet he didn't complain. And he only suggested stopping soon for the sake of the horse.

But that didn't mean I could rely on him. Not without knowing what was really going on inside his head.

The moon was rising when he finally pulled the wagon off the road at a point where there was a clearing under the trees. It was a well-chosen campsite, close to the road but out of sight behind a stand of overgrown thickets. If anything did come down that road hunting for us, we would have at least a little warning.

"I'll stay up and keep first watch. No arguments," I told him as we shared the last of my pastries and bread.

"No arguing," he said, raising his hands in half a motion of surrender.

"But I do have a few questions for you before you go to sleep," I said.

"Yeah, I figured you did," he said. "Can I start?"

"Go ahead," I said. Then I had to wait patiently as he fidgeted with the half-eaten roll in his hands and gathered his thoughts.

"I don't know what you know," he said at last. "But I'm going to guess that someone told you I've been coming to visit Esja."

"She mentioned it to me," I said.

"I know there are other men calling on her. Because she's a lovely, unmarried lady. But I wasn't there for those reasons," he said.

"Why were you there?" I asked.

He fidgeted with the roll some more, then deliberately set it aside, clasping his hands together between his knees. "I sensed something off about her. But I didn't know what it was. I thought maybe I was imagining it, or I would've said something to you. I mean, I was intending to say something to you, but later. After we were done cleaning up after the storm." Then he scoffed out a little laugh. "I guess I was planning on telling you yesterday or today, after you caught up on your sleep."

"Yeah, I missed doing that," I said with a dry laugh of my own. "So you're sure now that you weren't imagining it before?"

"No," he said with another chuckle at the irony. "But I suppose I have your perceptions to bolster mine, right?"

"What do you mean?" I asked.

"I know Esja was doing something at that well. I could feel it in the air. Like the tingling feeling before a thunderstorm. But I never saw a thing. But I'm guessing I wasn't imagining that something was going on?"

He looked up at me with equal measures of hope and agony in his eyes.

"No, something was going on," I told him. "But for my part, I don't think even I saw everything. I had the sense there was something down in that well that Esja was drawing up and spinning into magic that I *could* see. But I can't conjure an image of it in my mind or even in my drawing. It's like an un-thing."

"But you saw something?" he pressed.

"Well, the beacon that shot up into the sky was hard to miss," I said.

He scoffed again and shook his head. "I didn't see anything like that."

"No," I said, my mouth suddenly dry. "I don't suppose you would. But you did sense it."

"I sensed… something," was all he would admit.

I took a drink from my water bottle, then recapped it and put it back in my bag. Then I said, "You sensed something with Esja before she left town. That's more than I ever did. And I was looking. I was looking hard."

"I think it was like you said before. An un-thing," Roarr said. "I couldn't describe what I was feeling in words. But I guess that comes closest. Some un-thing was pulling at her. But it would hide. I felt like it hid, anyway, when Kara was near. I suppose it hid from you, too. I don't know. But I sensed something I couldn't prove was there. So I kept going back to see her. I don't know if I was hoping that feeling would go away, or if I was hoping it would get bigger, more perceptible."

"Either would've been an improvement, really," I said. "It's hard to know what to do with things that aren't quite there."

"I don't know that those feelings I was having ever got more focused," he said after another long moment's thought. "I just felt like, if I kept sensing them every time I saw her, it was time to tell you. But after you'd rested."

"Next time this comes up, grab me unrested if you have to," I said.

He laughed dutifully, but I hadn't really meant that as a joke.

"Okay, I have more questions," I said after letting him sit in silence for another passing of minutes.

"I'll answer, if I can," he said. But I could feel him tensing. Was that just nerves, or a preparation to guard against answering me honestly?

All I could do was ask. "You went to see Halldis," I said.

"Right," he said, nodding as if he had expected this question. Which, of course, he did. It was the obvious first question. "I got up yesterday morning and went to go see you. But you weren't at your house in town or at your cabin in the woods."

"I was at the Mikkelsens, helping to watch over Esja," I said.

For all the good I had done with that task.

But he just nodded. "Right, but I didn't know that. I didn't know where you were. And I was starting to panic a little. I mean, I still didn't know what exactly I was going to tell you. That I felt a thing that wasn't a thing and it was hanging around Esja? I don't know. But after checking your cabin, I decided to try your townhouse again."

"And I still wasn't there," I finished for him.

"No, but your cat was," he said. To my surprise.

"You saw Mjolner?" That was news to me. I mean, it wasn't the strangest thing for Mjolner to be at my house even when I wasn't. He didn't follow me around everywhere I went, especially if the only places I was going were in Villmark or in Runde.

But something about the way Roarr said it, I knew that he hadn't just had a chance encounter with my cat.

"I think he was waiting for me, actually," Roarr said. Since we had agreed not to chance drawing attention with a campfire, it was too dark for me to see if he was blushing. But he kind of sounded like he was.

"What did he do when he saw you?" I asked.

"He was sitting on one of the posts of your garden fence, and after I was done knocking on your door and was about to leave again, he just hopped down and started walking."

"With you?"

"No, before me. And I figured, maybe he wants me to follow him? So that's what I did."

And then it all clicked into place. How Roarr had gotten past Valki. How he had gotten through the stone blocking the access to Halldis's cave.

Mjolner had taken him the same as he had taken me. And he had never given me any hint of it.

But why?

"It's not like I wanted to see her. Ever. Again," Roarr said. His hands were still on his lap, but they were clenched into fists now, and his words came out through gritted teeth.

"Mjolner can be pretty persistent when he wants a human to do something," I said to him.

"I don't think I had to go," he said. "I could've turned and walked away. Maybe he would've found you instead. Maybe I should've done that."

"But you went to see her," I said. "How did she look to you?"

"Like she had when your grandmother condemned her," he said. "Well, maybe a little worse than that."

So she hadn't mustered any glamor, not even for the man she had held so long in her thrall.

Maybe she really was without any power anymore.

Or maybe she just wanted me to believe that.

"I asked her what was happening to Esja," Roarr said. "Well, I demanded she tell me. But she just laughed at me. She never said a single word, no matter what I said or did. She just laughed and laughed. I'm not sure what Mjolner thought I could accomplish down there, but I don't think I got it done."

"But you knew where Esja was going," I said.

"That was just another feeling, at least at first," he said. "I was leaving the cave. By myself. Mjolner disappeared after letting me out of her cave, like he needed to go find you or anyone else who could do a better job than I had done. But I was walking back up towards the surface when something just clicked in my mind."

Which explained why, when he'd run back out, that Valki had seen him. Mjolner hadn't been with him that time.

I'd have to remember to tell Valki when I saw him next. I was still going to do everything I could to take some of the weight off his shoulders. But he needed to know he hadn't fallen down in his duty the way he thought he had.

My cat could be as devious as Loke when he wanted to be.

"What clicked?" I asked when I realized Roarr had lapsed back into silence.

"Esja was getting stronger, and Halldis was looking very weak," he said. "That has to be related, doesn't it?"

Well, he'd come to that conclusion faster than I had.

Although I still wasn't positive it was correct. It *could* just be a coincidence. It would be just like Halldis to employ the opportunity such a coincidence would present to sow confusion in my mind. To make me jump to false conclusions.

"But how did that bring you here?" I asked.

"That village," Roarr said, in a whisper, as if afraid the village itself could overhear us despite the miles we'd already put between us and it. "It's where she's from. Originally."

"And by originally, you mean decades ago," I said. "A lot of decades ago."

"That's where she sent me, to find things for her," he said, still in a whisper. "Most of the things she sent me to find were gone. Almost all of them, really. I've spent more time digging through the remains of those houses than I want to think about now."

"But that's not where the amulet was from," I said.

"No, that was a campsite on the side of the road. Kind of like this one, actually. But it wasn't on this road," he said. "But I think, possibly, the charm that man used to summon the Wild Hunt came from here. That village is a very dangerous place."

"And it's just been rendered far more dangerous by what happened today," I said with a sigh. Although I had my doubts about the Wild Hunt summoning charm. My gut sense was that whoever had given it to the Villmarker man who had used it had been from much further north.

"But what about Esja? Is she going to be okay?" he asked.

"I don't know," I admitted. "I can take a look at her when we're home again. But I think we'll need your help."

"My help?" He sounded genuinely surprised.

"You seem more sensitive to the un-thing than I am," I said. "Or maybe you're right and it hides from me. In which case, I don't stand much of a chance of ever detecting its presence. But perhaps you can help me sense it. And if you're the only one who can sense it, I'm going to need you all the more then."

"This isn't exactly the responsibility I was looking for," he said, looking down at his own hands.

But, I noticed, he didn't turn it down.

CHAPTER TWENTY-THREE

ᚺ

Roarr went to bed soon after, curling up inside his sleeping bag on the wagon floor in the corner around the pedestal leg of the tiny table.

The wagon was a tight space for three. There was no getting around that.

Esja slept on in the wagon's only bunk, her breath deep and even.

I hoped all that was happening was that she was sleeping off the exhaustion of channeling a lot of raw power. She might be stronger now than she'd ever been before, but that sort of magical effort demanded training. It was like running a marathon after a lifetime of not walking further than from the couch to the refrigerator.

It was a lot.

I sat in the open door at the back of the wagon, keeping an eye on our sleeping horse and also the road beyond. The horse was only a darker patch of shadow under the trees to my eyes, but the road itself shone brightly, the whitish stones glowing like liquid silver in the moonlight.

From where I sat, I could see more than a mile both to the northwest and to the southeast. Nothing was going to sneak up on us.

I was turning the pages of my sketchbook, more as an exercise to stay awake than out of any real hope of discovering some new useful detail by the little bit of moonlight that reached me through the tree-tops above, when I heard Esja's breathing suddenly changed.

She sucked in a deep breath, like someone surfacing after a long dive. Then she sat up in the bunk. She was just short enough to do that without hitting her head, although barely.

But her posture was odd. Too straight. Too tense.

Then she opened her eyes. Only all I could see were the whites of her sclera. They caught glimmers of moonlight, but that only made the whole effect that much more eerie.

"Esja?" I said, setting my book aside to turn towards her.

Roarr, on the floor, slept on.

So did the horse.

But Esja turned her face, not all the way towards me but halfway. Like she could hear me but not see me, and only had a vague idea of my location.

Then she spoke. To my relief, it was her voice I heard, not that growling creature speaking through her. And her words were in clear, modern Villmarker Norse.

"Torfa drove her out of Villmark," Esja said. Her cadence was as if she was resuming a story only briefly interrupted. And I wondered how much I had missed. Like who this "her" was, for starters.

But I wasn't about to interrupt. I leaned closer to be sure I didn't miss a word as she went on.

"She had sown mischief between the men, and she didn't deny it. But she swore to Torfa she would have her revenge. For they were equally matched in power. The only difference between them was that Torfa had the love of the people, and the Golden One did not."

I still didn't interrupt, but I did scramble to grab my book and a pencil from my bag. I had to write this story down. But even as I raced to get down the words, my mind was already wondering if Haraldr knew this story already.

If he had a book about it.

Or if my ancestors, the Torfudottirs, had kept this story to themselves. I would have to ask my grandmother about that.

"The Golden One knew herself well. She knew she thrived on

chaos. But she wasn't ashamed. She loved stirring things up. It keeps life exciting. Yet Torfa, who loved order above all things, was determined to destroy the Golden One. Because she disrupted the order. The order that put Torfa above all things."

I felt a chill run up my spine as I copied those words down. I had briefly touched the spirit of Torfa through her ancestral fire. The true, powerful one that was hidden in an inaccessible cavern deep beneath Villmark, not the lesser one Valki and the Mikkelsens kept guard over.

It had not been a pleasant experience.

But I had also felt the power of chaos, just that afternoon. And I was hoping not to revisit that ever again, either.

I hoped whatever fight that Esja was relaying a tale of to me now, it wasn't one I'd ever be expected to take sides in.

But I was pretty sure I was already a part of it. My side had been chosen for me.

And I had chosen it again when I had taken up the mantle of volva in training.

"She was driven out, the Golden One was, so she founded her own village. And those who weren't welcome in Torfa's domain found a home in hers. But Torfa could not tolerate the existence of a home for those she had driven out. And especially not for the Golden One. So she sent her fiercest warriors to put an end to the matter."

"They burned her," I guessed. It had been the faintest of whispers under my breath as I scribbled away.

But it drew Esja's attention to me. Those white eyes were fixed on me now.

"They burned her," she said. "Three times they burned her. They burned her once, and she was Urd. They burned her a second time, and she was Skuld. They burned her a third time, and she was Verdande."

This story I knew. It was in the Edda. Only it had been about Gullveig, who had come between the Aesir and the Vanir in Norse mythology.

Was Esja talking about the same myth? Gull meant gold. And Gullveig had nearly caused a ruinous war between the two tribes of gods, the Aesir and the Vanir. But Odin had speared her, and then she was burned.

Three times.

And each time, another of the Norns had emerged from the flames. First Urd, who was the past. Then Skuld, who was what was yet to come. Then Verdande, the ever-changing present.

But surely if where all that had taken place actually had a location in this world, it would be back in the Old World. In Norway or Sweden. Not here. Not in Minnesota, inside a pocket world defined by the spells that held Torfa's people hidden away from the rest of the world.

And yet. It certainly sounded like what Esja was talking about.

"Urd was first," she said.

And I said, not bothering to whisper this time. "The spinner of threads." Urd was associated with Hagall, the rune I had been struggling to bond with. Urd was also the name of the wellspring that provided the water the Norns used to mend the dragon-chewed roots of the World Tree.

I had so many more questions for the next time I saw Haraldr. They all clamored at my mind.

But chiefest among them: what did Urd spin the threads *from*?

"Yes," Esja said to me with the smallest of nods. "Then Skuld."

"And then Verdande," I said, nodding along with her.

But she fixed those sightless eyes on me again. And when she said, "Next Skuld," there was no question in my mind.

She was delivering a threat.

Whatever Skuld's arrival would mean, it wouldn't be good for the people of Villmark.

And I would have to prepare for it.

I hadn't been prepared for Urd at all. Those threads had been woven. I had buried them down at the bottom of the well, but I hadn't unmade them.

If anything else could move those stones, everything she had woven would go back up into the sky again.

And then what? More hailstorms like the last?

Or worse?

But Esja, apparently, had said her piece. She snapped her head back until she was facing forward, closed her eyes, and collapsed back onto the bunk.

There was an agonizingly long period of absolute quiet. I couldn't even hear insects or amphibians in the woods around us. I wasn't sure what exactly I was listening for, but I knew I wasn't hearing it. And I could feel panic rising inside me.

Then Esja took another deep breath like a surfaced diver. And the moment broke. The whirring and croaking of the little creatures of the forest were there again, just as they should be.

Esja didn't wake. She just turned on her side, curled up, and slipped back to sleep.

But it was a more normal sleep than before. And I was certain that when Roarr and I rose at sunrise, she would get up with us.

Perhaps she'd even be her normal self again. Although I was going to have to accept that the new, vivacious, flirty version of Esja *was* the normal Esja.

But I would have to be doubly sure someone was always with her. Because I didn't think her own story was done yet.

No, I was pretty sure we'd only completed the first of three chapters.

CHAPTER TWENTY-FOUR

ᚺ

THE NEXT DAY I rode on the back of the top of the wagon again, legs dangling over the door as I sketched in my book. I wasn't drawing much in particular.

But mostly because my brain wasn't letting me slip into a fugue state. I couldn't draw in my usual magic way. But I was pretty sure that was just because I was so very tired.

Soon we'd be back in Villmark. And I could go home and sleep for twelve solid hours.

Or so I hoped. But not with any real expectation of it coming true.

Esja couldn't go back to the Mikkelsens now. And she couldn't go back to stay with Sigvin. She was my entire responsibility. Until I knew what was happening with her and how to keep her and everyone else safe from whatever that was, she would have to stay close to me. All the time.

It doubled my exhaustion, just thinking about it. I didn't know how I was going to watch over her, continue my studies, and continue my work as volva all at once. It didn't seem possible.

But as I rocked with the motion of the wagon, I could hear snippets of the conversation that Roarr was having with Esja.

She had, indeed, woken up that morning seemingly entirely normal.

Well, she'd been a little upset at first. She didn't know where she was or why Roarr and I were there with her, inside Kara's and Thorge's wagon.

And she had no memory at all of anything that had happened since the day before last, when she'd been trying on outfits to wear to my grandmother's mead hall. For our night out.

But she did remember sneaking out to Aldís's mead hall on multiple occasions. Although she seemed pretty embarrassed about it when Roarr gently teased her.

"I just like to dance," Esja said, punching him lightly in the arm. "And I like to have people watching me dance. And to have people dancing with me. Why does everyone seem to think that all I want is to stay quietly at home and paint?"

"You seemed happy enough to do that before," Roarr said. "Or was that only because you were unwell so much of the time?"

"I like painting," she said. She was talking more softly now, leaning closer to Roarr's shoulder as the wagon lurched over ruts in the road. She wasn't exactly trying to speak so that I couldn't hear her, but I did have to focus a little harder to catch her words.

"You are very good at it," Roarr told her. In a level tone of voice that said he was only stating facts, not trying to flatter her.

"And I did like being home," she said after a smiling pause.

"Did you? You seemed so eager to be away," he said. Still with the same level tone. Like he wasn't judging her.

"Where I've been staying in town isn't my home," she said, speaking more softly again, so I had to lean back a little to hear her. "I meant my actual home. Down in the valley south of town."

"Loke should've fixed it up for the two of you," Roarr said. "If you like, we can fix it up for you now."

"You can?" she said, stressing the first word ever so slightly. He chuckled, not remotely offended.

"Well, I can see that it gets done," he said. "And I can help. But, yeah, you're right. I've not exactly taken up the family line of being a builder of things."

"You could, though," she said.

"I don't think that's my life's work. But I can certainly do my part to fix up your house. If you like," he said again. Clearly, he meant it as a question.

"Let me think about it," she said.

"I didn't mean to upset you," Roarr said.

"Do I sound upset?" she asked.

"A little," he said.

"I guess my feelings about that house are complicated," she said. "I was hoping never to go back there again. I think I was afraid if I did, I'd be trapped there all over again. And everything that's happened since I moved into Villmark would be like a dream, fading every day until I couldn't remember it at all."

"I'd still come visit you," he said. "If you did go back."

"Would you?" she asked teasingly.

"If you wanted me to," he said. "It's not such a bad place, that house. Just a little worse for the wear."

"I guess I still think so too," she said. But I could tell by the sound of her voice that she was smiling at him again. "I do love that house. And I know it loves me. It has always been there to take care of me. Even before my parents died, I knew that house was my chief protector."

"Is the house happy as it is?" Roarr asked. Perfectly seriously. "Would fixing it up make the house unhappy?"

I was taking Esja seriously, too. I cocked an ear in her direction to wait to hear what she said next, even as I turned back the pages of my sketchbook. To find the drawings I had done of her house.

"I don't know," Esja said. "But I think if I ask, it will answer. Not with words, obviously. But I'll know what it wants. If I ask and then listen."

"I think that's likely true," Roarr agreed.

The two of them fell silent then, and I was vaguely aware of Esja resting her head on Roarr's shoulder as he held the reins and drove us all home.

I tried to decide if that was worrying. But with the alternatives being the likes of Raggi or Skefill, I decided that if Roarr was her new favorite, I could live with that.

Mjolner trusted him. That meant a lot to me. Even if that cat hadn't bothered to clue me in on that fact.

And I could see no reason for Roarr to have gone after Esja except to save her, and by extension to save all of Villmark. And he had known how dangerous the power was that she was messing with.

He had risked, not just his life, but more. He had risked being in something's thrall again. He couldn't have relished that thought.

But he had never stopped running towards that risk. To get to Esja in time.

I had no idea what Loke would think of it all. But he wasn't here. And Esja couldn't put her life on hold, waiting for him to come back.

None of us could.

I stopped turning the pages of my sketchbook at some of the drawings I had done after Esja had given me permission to enter the house.

I hadn't seen anything in them before. I had intended to look again, after I was better rested. Which, after keeping watch for more than half the night, I definitely wasn't now.

But sometimes being so tired that hallucinations were a real danger could help. It was like looking with new eyes, anyway.

So I looked.

And I did see some things I hadn't noticed before. Little details in the background, only the faintest of lines, but I was sure I wasn't hallucinating.

There were runes there, in the pencil lines. Bind runes. And once runes had been overlapped into bind runes, it wasn't always easy to guess all the runes that had formed that bind rune.

My drawings were getting harder to interpret the more runes I got acquainted with. Because they all tended to show up to a greater or lesser extent. And they were more and more overlapping into bind runes that took even more work to pick apart and search for meaning.

I longed for the old days when all I saw in a drawing of Loke's and

Esja's house was an overwhelming sense of inverted Fe, of a lack of material wealth. So simple. So clear.

But as I touched my fingertip to the graphite on the page, I got a sense of what Esja had been talking about.

The house wasn't exactly a living thing. And it certainly didn't have a mind of its own.

It didn't strike me as a thing of latent power like some of the artifacts of old magic I had encountered, either.

No, it was more like after serving as a home for generations of their family, it had acquired a patina of their family's hamingja. Which was a Norse concept kind of like karma, except in all the ways that it isn't like that at all.

Hamingja is carried through families, and everyone in that family has a fate colored by their collective hamingja. But they can also affect that hamingja by their own actions, for good or ill.

Family honor was part of it. But there was more individualism in the Norse way of thinking of that concept. Individual actions mattered.

You were born to a family with a certain reputation and an obligation to do all you could to improve it or, if it was already sky-high, to live up to it. To do otherwise was to condemn your offspring to a diminished starting point.

Loke didn't much like talking about these things. Not about his own family. Ever.

And I wasn't sure that Esja knew enough about such esoteric concepts to talk about them with me, either.

But she, like Roarr, had a gut sense of things that even I with all my training struggled to see.

Anyway, looking at the runes clustered in my drawings, I felt what she had felt. The house, infused with the hamingja of her family, protected her. It kept her safe.

She had been in the center of that hailstorm, but that house had kept her safe from all of it. It hadn't shown a bit of damage, even to itself. That was some strong protective magic.

But then I turned to a sketch I had drawn in her bedroom, and saw other things.

The runes in the woodwork of the walls around her bed were gathered in bind runes. Bind runes of protection. Not quite actual wards like my grandmother deployed, but powerful all the same.

Powerful enough that they had hid from my eyes in my own drawing when I had first looked at them, still standing in her house. Inside the reach of those bind runes. Every time I'd looked since it had been in poor light, but I really should've noticed them that first time around. They had hid from me on purpose.

But I didn't sense that purpose was malicious. Those runes just wanted to keep Esja safe.

But safe to them meant in that bed. Not out in the world.

And yet, I wasn't getting a smothering helicopter parent vibe from it, either.

I couldn't point to a single thing in that picture to back it up, but my gut sense was very strong that the house had been keeping her sick. Not through radon or black mold or some rare genetic disorder yet to be discovered.

It had kept her sick through the magic of its carefully ordered runes.

Because keeping her just sick enough to remain housebound had kept her safe.

Almost as if it, or they, or whatever infused the house, had known that an Esja who was strong and well was an Esja that was going to be lured by the darkness that had, indeed, gotten to her in the end.

One thing that was becoming clear to me, though, was that there was a very real possibility that raw chaos like what Esja had pulled from the well wasn't the only kind of power I couldn't see or perceive.

And just because I couldn't see it didn't mean it was bad, either. It didn't even mean it was trying to hide from me or the eyes of others like my grandmother. It just was, by its nature, hidden.

Then I sucked in a breath as that thought finally clicked into place in my mind. Unseen, hidden, secret. Dark.

And from the motherly way it was trying to protect Esja from outside forces, I would call it feminine.

And here I'd thought the dark feminine was the thing making Esja behave strangely, or was the thing trying to lure her out of town.

I had been looking at the house the whole time, but never seeing its role in everything.

I shut my sketchbook and put it away. I was going to want to think this all over more carefully later. After that twelve hours of sleep.

And then I was going to talk to my grandmother about everything that had happened.

And then I was going to do the same thing again, but with Haraldr.

And then I was going to research, not only what had happened in the first days of the settlement when Torfa had yet lived and ruled, if any records from that time still existed.

I also needed to know a lot more about Loke's and Esja's family.

If Loke were here, he'd absolutely keep me from doing just that.

But he wasn't here. And I needed to know.

I suspected that learning about Esja and what was going on with her was going to risk learning more about Loke and what was going on with him. And he really wouldn't like that at all.

But he wasn't here.

And I really did need to know.

My thoughts were truly on a glum path, but then our wagon turned around the last bend and onto the straightaway that would lead us out of the woods and into Villmark proper.

And waiting for me just at the edge of those woods was Mjolner. But he wasn't in his usual carefully arranged pose with his tail wrapped around his paws. He wasn't washing his ears as if he'd been waiting there for me for hours.

No, he was wavering on his feet as if he were standing on the deck of a ship on high seas. And the minute we came around the bend and he saw us approaching, it was like he couldn't fight to remain standing for a second more.

He collapsed to the ground on his side and didn't stir.

CHAPTER TWENTY-FIVE

I JUMPED down from the wagon and ran to Mjolner's side.

He was breathing, but he only opened one eye partway to look up at me. It was like his head was too heavy for him to lift.

I scooped him up and carried him into the wagon.

"Can we do anything to help?" Roarr asked as he held the door open for me and helped me up the step and through the doorway.

"No, just get me home as quickly as you can," I said.

He nodded and closed the door. I felt the wagon sway as he swung back up into the driver's seat. Then we were underway once more.

We were nearly home. I knew it.

And yet, if it had been possible to make the wagon go faster, I would gladly have gotten out and pushed.

"What happened to you, Mjolner?" I asked as I laid him down on the pillow.

He meowed weakly, but closed his eyes. No slow blinks for me today.

I stroked his black fur, then noticed his paws.

The skin there was blue. Very dark blue. Like he'd gotten frostbite on the pads of his paws. I warmed them between my hands as best as I could.

How had he gotten frostbite on such a hot August day?

But I already knew the answer to that question. He had been in the north, far in the north, looking for Loke and Thorbjorn. Because I had sent him there.

Had they truly gone so far north that there was still ice on the ground?

"You didn't find them, did you?" I said softly. Because if he had, he wouldn't have come back alone.

But he didn't answer. Although he did purr, ever so softly, as I warmed his paws.

I could hear the sounds of the town through the walls of the wagon and knew we were back in Villmark. When Roarr finally brought the horse to a halt, I was already on my feet with Mjolner in my arms, ready to jump down out of the wagon and head into the house.

"What can we do?" Esja asked as she followed me through my garden gate and to my front door.

"You stay with me," I said to her, perhaps a bit more firmly than she needed to hear it. She bit her lip, and I saw hurt in her eyes, but she nodded without a word.

"And me?" Roarr asked.

"Bring my bags inside for me, would you?" I said to him as I carried Mjolner into my kitchen. I pushed a few of the gift baskets out of the way so I could lay him down on the counter. "Then bring the wagon back to Kara and see to the horse. Extra apples for the hard word."

"Of course," he said. But he was still lingering uncertainly in the kitchen doorway. "And then?"

"Then straight back here," I told him. "We still have work to do."

"Of course," he said again, but with more enthusiasm this time. I heard him go out the door, then return a short time later to set the bags in the mudroom with a soft thump. And then he was gone.

But he would be back. And the two of us were going to have a long conversation.

"I've put some water on the stove," Esja said, even as she appeared at my elbow with a folded towel. Not a kitchen towel, but one of the fluffy ones from my bathroom up the stairs.

"Thank you," I said, picking Mjolner up long enough for her to spread the towel under him.

"I don't get out much, but I know how to treat frostbite," she said. "Do you think he wants some food?"

"Open one of the cans of sardines in that cupboard over there," I said.

He didn't stir at the word "sardines" like he usually did. But his eyes burst open when he heard Esja turning the key to open the can. And he lifted his head, ready for a taste, even before she'd returned to the table.

She fed him bits of fish while I filled a basin with the now warm water and then put Mjolner's paws into it.

"It doesn't look too bad," I said. "I don't think he lost any flesh. Nothing is sloughing off, anyway. I think he'll be okay."

"I'm sure he knew to come back before it got too bad," Esja said as she held another piece of sardine out on her fingertips for Mjolner to lick away.

"I'm sorry. I sent him to find Thorbjorn, so Thorbjorn could decide whether or not to tell your brother what was going on with you," I said.

"Don't be sorry," Esja said with a shaky smile. "I don't remember what happened myself, but to hear Roarr tell it, I looked pretty scary. Of course you thought he had to know."

"Right," I said, deciding I didn't need to explain the timing of sending Mjolner on his mission to her. "But I meant, I'm sorry because if Mjolner is here now and alone, that means he didn't find them."

"I think they're okay," Esja said after a moment's thought. "I mean, I think I'd sense it, if something had happened to Loke. Don't you feel the same?"

"I don't always sense everything I should," I admitted.

"I'm sorry. For my part in that," she said.

"Were you hiding things from me?" I asked her.

"No, I wasn't," she said. "I guess whatever Roarr sees happening around me, it kind of links up to times where I find myself doing things really impulsively. Like jumping out of windows, or throwing things at Nilda."

Saying that last bit brought a deep blush to her cheeks. But she pressed on.

"I don't feel like I was ever not me," she said. "But maybe I can't trust my own feelings, either."

"Roarr can see things even I can't," I said. "I hope it's all right with you if I ask him to stay here."

"With you?" she asked with a confused frown.

"Oh, sorry. I guess I've been inside my own head so long, I've forgotten we've not actually had this conversation," I said. "With *us*. I need you to stay close beside me."

"So you can watch me," she said.

"So I can watch over you," I corrected.

"You have enough room?" she asked.

"There are three bedrooms upstairs. I only use the one," I said. "You'll take the middle room, so Roarr can have the one at the top of the stairs."

"So he can watch over me too," she said.

"Well, yes," I said. "I'm afraid the only other option is something in the caves. But I don't think that's going to do any of us any good."

"Wouldn't everyone be safer if I was locked up?" she asked.

"No," I said. "I really don't. First of all, you might not even have that thing inside you anymore. Roarr and I saw you throw all the magic down to the bottom of the well, and I trapped it down there. It could be that the problem has already been dealt with. Certainly you've shown no signs of any lingering effects since then."

"Yeah," Esja said, stirring idly at the oil at the bottom of the empty sardine can with a single fingertip. "But you don't believe that."

"Well, you sat up in the middle of sleeping last night and told me a long story about the Norns, so I have a hunch you might do some other things. Two more times," I said.

"I was talking in my sleep?" she asked. "Or something was talking through me?"

"It sounded like you," I said.

She nodded, but said nothing. Then she turned, put the sardine can in the trashcan under my sink, then washed the fish and oil off her hands.

I lifted Mjolner back out of the basin and dried off his paws one by one. He licked at them a little fussily, but he seemed in better shape than when I had found him.

I cuddled him in my arms, then carried him into the living room to lay him down in the fancy cat bed by the fireplace that Nilda and Kara had given us as a housewarming present when I'd first moved into Villmark so many months before.

"I want to help you, any way I can," Esja said from the kitchen doorway. "If you want me to stay inside this house and never leave it, I'll do that. Any spells you want to try, or bindings, or anything. I want to help."

"I don't intend to keep you prisoner," I told her. "But for now, we'll say the only rule is you should always be with either me or Roarr. You can go out, but one of us has to be with you. Agreed?"

"Agreed," she said. She disappeared down the hallway towards the mudroom, but came back again. She had my art bag and my duffel bag. But she also had her own bag with all the clothes she had packed to take with her when she'd left the Mikkelsens.

"I have things still at Nilda's and Kara's," she said. "And some things at Sigvin's, too."

"We'll have it all brought here," I said.

She nodded again, then gestured towards the stairs. "Do you mind if I settle in my room? Take a bath? Sleep for a million years?"

"Make yourself at home," I said.

She managed an actual smile at that, then went up the stairs, turning down the corridor that led to the bedrooms and disappearing from my view.

I sat on the floor by the cat bed, stroking Mjolner's fur and waiting for Roarr to return.

I didn't have to wait long. And when he came in, he had his own pack with him.

Like he already knew what I was going to ask of him.

"You don't mind?" I asked.

"I want to do what I can, and this is what I can do," he said with a shrug. "I just wished I understood better what's happening."

So I told him the parts he didn't know, about Esja's tale from her sleep talking episode, and about her house, and just a little about my fears for Loke and Thorbjorn.

"I'm sure they'll be back," he said. "If not as soon as we'd all like."

"I miss them both," I said. For different reasons, obviously.

But then I added, because it was true, "But I'm glad you're here with me."

"Well," he said, and went red straight to the tips of his ears. Which I could see because he was hunched over now, hands deep in his pockets as he studied his own feet. He seemed to cast about for something else to say, and landed on, "I don't understand about Esja's house, though. It's haunted?"

"Not exactly," I said. "I'll probably have to go out there a few more times to look at some things. But Esja can't go back there. Not until I understand more."

"Sure, I can watch her while you're out," he said. "But what do you *think* is going on with it?"

"I think there is power in Loke's and Esja's family line. Old power," I said. "My grandmother has taught me to see our sort of magic, volva magic, but Loke told me once—"

But I broke off with a gasp as I remembered just what Loke had said to me, shortly after I had met him, almost a year before.

"What?" Roarr asked, looking quite alarmed as I just sat there with my hand over my mouth, gaping at him.

I pulled myself together.

"This was just after we dealt with Halldis. My first days in Villmark," I said. "I was telling Loke that my grandmother didn't like it when he told me things about magic and the history of the town and all that. Because she said I would have to unlearn what he taught me before I could learn properly."

"That sounds like something she would say," Roarr said diplomatically.

"Yes, but then Loke offered to teach me himself."

"Teach you what?" he asked with a crease forming between this furrowed brows.

"Teach me a different sort of magic," I said. "I remember now. He said my grandmother's magic was too binding. Too confining. Too many rules. And he could teach me to reach for another source of power."

"Do you think he was offering you *chaos*? Like what was in that well?" Roarr asked. I could tell he was struggling not to sound skeptical.

But I was skeptical too. Or, at least, I wanted to be.

"He's not brought it up since," was all I could say.

"He might have been messing with you," Roarr said. "Especially since this was when you were still new here. If he's not said anything like it since, after all the things the two of you have done together, I would think that points to the fact he was just messing with you."

"But what did he go north to find?" I asked.

Roarr scratched the back of his neck as he mulled that over. But then just gave me a shrug. "If it was chaos he was after, I suspect he already knew it was at the bottom of that well. You were both there before."

"It seemed like a new place to him when he brought me there," I mused. "He had to use my own sketch as a way in. Not that I remotely understand how his power works. And yet, what if it does come from chaos?"

"Do you even know where his power came from?" Roarr asked.

"Not really. I think he bargained with something. For the sake of his sister. But now he's gone, and she left that house, and her protection is all gone. I'm afraid for what's going to happen next with her."

"We'll watch out for her," Roarr said, lifting his chin as if taking a vow. Which he kind of was. "Whoever or whatever this Golden One is, we won't give her another chance to take Esja from us. We'll protect her. Together."

I nodded glumly. The words sounded good. Of course they did.

I was just afraid the reality was going to fall short. Maybe by a lot.

But then Mjolner stirred under my hand. He sat up with only a little bit of a struggle, more as if long napping had left him cramping than as if his injured paws were hurting him.

Then he looked at me, then at Roarr, and then back at me.

And he gave me a slow blink of his bright yellow-green eyes.

I blinked back at him.

And so did Roarr. Almost with reverence.

And just like that, I knew. I knew that Esja was going to be all right. Roarr and I had saved her from the first attempt to burn her. And we would save her again, two more times.

And I could only imagine who Esja would be after emerging from that trifold experience. But I knew she'd be all the stronger for it.

Who she would be when her brother finally returned to town was bound to be impressive. But she would discover that person for herself. Roarr and I were just there to make sure she could do it.

And that was really what my calling to be a volva meant. I kept everyone in Villmark safe from the darkness all around us. So they could build their own lives as they saw fit.

As callings go, it's a good one. I was glad it was mine.

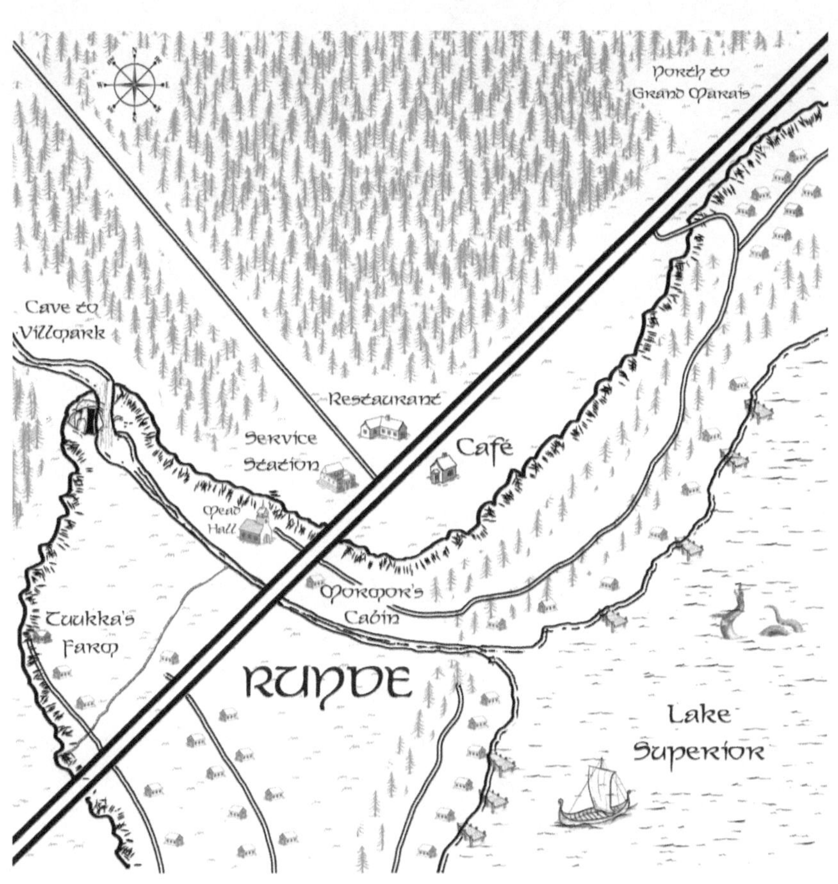

North to
Grand Marais
Cave to
Villmark
Restaurant
Service
Station
Café
Mead
Hall
Mormor's
Cabin
Tuukka's
Farm
RUNDE
Lake
Superior

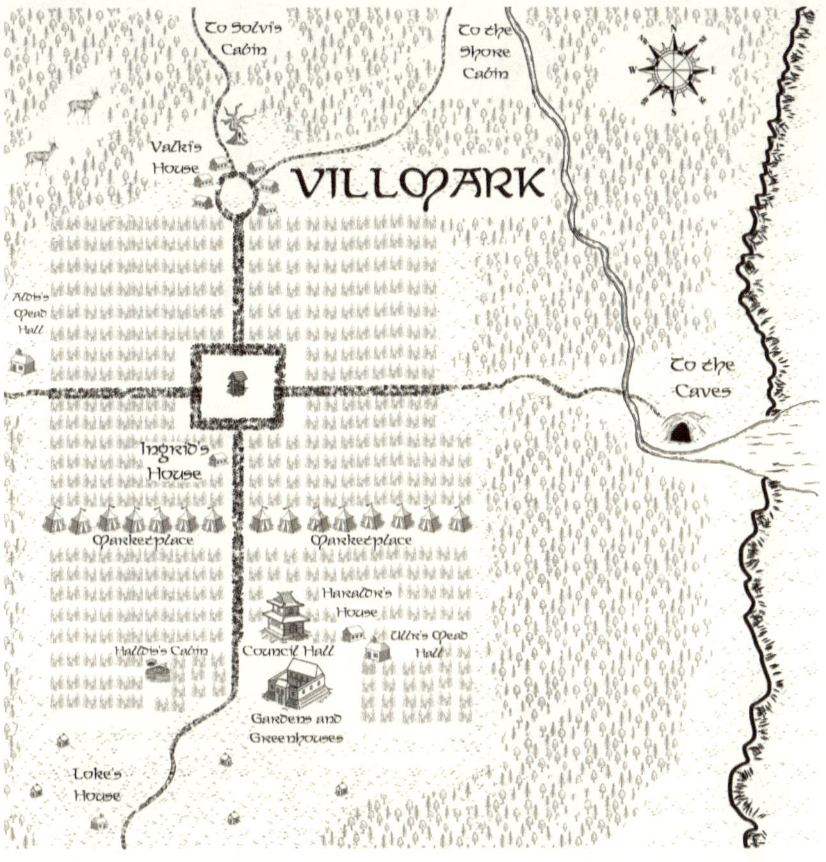

To Solvi's Cabin
To the Shore Cabin
N
W E
S
Valki's House
VILLMARK
Aldi's Mead Hall
To the Caves
Ingrid's House
Marketplace
Marketplace
Harald's House
Halldis's Cabin
Council Hall
Ullr's Mead Hall
Gardens and Greenhouses
Loke's House

CHECK OUT BOOK THIRTEEN!

The Viking Witch will return in Predator in the Lanes, available now!

Ingrid Torfudottir moved to the North Shore of Lake Superior intending to live with her grandmother while pursuing a career as a book illustrator. Instead, she discovered her true calling as a volva—a Viking witch—serving a village founded in the Viking age by Norse settlers escaping some terrible enemy whose identity was lost to time.

Now she lives in the hidden town of Villmark full-time. Her boyfriend Thorbjorn and her best friend Loke remain in the wilds far to the north of Villmark, their fates a mystery to those they left behind. Like Ingrid.

And like Esja, Loke's sister. Ingrid awaits the next evolution of Esja's destiny, so intertwined with her own. What happens next will test them both.

But then the unexpected occurs. Something preys on the women of Villmark, killing them in the very streets of the town. And Ingrid and Esja both swear to catch this predator before it strikes again.

Predator in the Lanes, the thirteen book in **The Viking Witch Mystery Series**!

THE WITCHES THREE
COZY MYSTERIES

In case you missed it, check out **Charm School**, the first book in the complete **Witches Three Cozy Mystery Series**!

Amanda Clarke thinks of herself as perfectly ordinary in every way. Just a small-town girl who serves breakfast all day in a little diner nestled next to the highway, nothing but dairy farms for miles around. She fits in there.

But then an old woman she never met dies, and Amanda was named in her will. Now Amanda packs a bag and heads to the big city, to Miss Zenobia Weekes' Charm School for Exceptional Young Ladies. And it's not in just any neighborhood. No, she finds herself on Summit Avenue in St. Paul, a street lined with gorgeous old houses, the former homes of lumber barons, railroad millionaires, even the writer F. Scott Fitzgerald. Why, Amanda can practically hear the jazz music still playing across the decades.

Scratch that. The music really, literally, still plays in the backyard of the charm school. Because the house stretches across time itself. Without a witch to protect this tear in the fabric of the world, anything can spill over. Like music.

Or like murder.

Charm School, the first book in the complete **Witches Three Cozy Mystery Series!**

THE WEAL & WOE BOOKSHOP
WITCH MYSTERIES

In case you missed it, check out **The Teashop Terror**, the first book in the complete **Weal & Woe Bookshop Witch Mystery Series**!

No one knows more about every branch of magic than Tabitha Greene. She devoted years to studying the most esoteric texts, hunting down the most obscure source materials, and deciphering the most cryptic ancient scrolls. But her career in academia hits a dead end when no wizard will take her on as an apprentice.

Just because, despite being descended from two long and prestigious lines of witches, her attempts to actually perform any magic always fail. Often spectacularly.

But no more college means no more dorm life. And no magical skills means no real job skills, at least, not in the witchy world. And a life spent moving from school to school every few months was a life without real friendships. She finds herself alone with nowhere to go.

Then an uncle she barely remembers offers her a summer job, running his bookstore over the summer. The Weal and Woe Bookstore, located in a magical pocket world within a block of buildings just north of the old Mill District of Minneapolis, Minnesota.

Not exactly the pinnacle of all her hopes and dreams. But it's just for one summer, right?

Or so Tabitha tells herself. But unbeknownst to her, the Weal and Woe Bookstore is about to change her life.

The Teashop Terror, the first book in the complete **Weal & Woe Bookshop Witch Mystery Series**!

The Ritchie and Fitz Sci-Fi Murder Mysteries starts with **Murder on the Intergalactic Railway**.

For Murdina Ritchie, acceptance at the Oymyakon Foreign Service Academy means one last chance at her dream of becoming a diplomat for the Union of Free Worlds. For Shackleton Fitz IV, it represents his last chance not to fail out of military service entirely.

Strange that fate should throw them together now, among the last group of students admitted after the start of the semester. They had once shared the strongest of friendships. But that all ended a long time ago.

But when an insufferable but politically important woman turns up murdered, the two agree to put their differences aside and work together to solve the case.

Because the murderer might strike again. But more importantly, solving a murder would just have to impress the dour colonel who clearly thinks neither of them belong at his academy.

Murder on the Intergalactic Railway, the first book in **The Ritchie**

and Fitz Sci-Fi Murder Mysteries, available everywhere books are sold.

FREE EBOOK!

Like exclusive, free content?

If you'd like to receive "A Collection of Witchy Prequels", a free collection of short story prequels to the Witches Three Cozy Mystery and Viking Witch Mystery series, as well as other free stories throughout the year, go to my website CateMartin.com to subscribe to my newsletter! This eBook is exclusively for newsletter subscribers and will never be sold in stores. Check it out!

ABOUT THE AUTHOR

Cate Martin has written stories which have appeared in **Mystery, Crime and Mayhem** quarterly magazine as well as in the annual **Holiday Spectacular** Advent calendar of Christmas stories. She is also the author of three witch mystery series: **The Witches Three Cozy Mysteries**, and **The Viking Witch Mysteries** and **The Weal and Woe Bookshop Witch Mysteries**. She currently lives in Minneapolis, Minnesota. You can learn more about her work at CateMartin.com.

ALSO BY CATE MARTIN

The Witches Three Cozy Mystery Series

Charm School

Work Like a Charm

Third Time is a Charm

Old World Charm

Charm his Pants Off

Charm Offensive

The Witches Three Cozy Mysteries Books 1-3

The Witches Three Cozy Mysteries Books 4-6

The Viking Witch Mystery Series

Body at the Crossroads

Death Under the Bridge

Murder on the Lake

Killing in the Village Commons

Bloodshed in the Forest

Corpse in the Mead Hall

Slaying on the Lake Shore

Bones by the Forest Road

Sacrifice Behind the Falls

Body Under the Café

Assassination in the Glade

Bewitchment After the Storm

Predator in the Lanes

Threat From the North

Snare in the Blind Alley

Ashes Beneath the Tree (available July 14, 2026 direct from me or August 11, 2026 in stores everywhere)

The Viking Witch Mysteries Books 1-3

The Viking Witch Mysteries Books 4-6

The Viking Witch Mysteries Books 7-9

The Weal & Woe Bookshop Witch Mystery Series

The Teashop Terror

The Salon & Spa Scandal

The Bookseller Blunder

The Entrepreneur Enigma

The Novelty Shop Nightmare

The Courtyard Conundrum

Short Story Collections

Bubbly, Bicycles and Brides

The Dorothy Lundegaard Mysteries

Fruitcake, Festivities and Firelight

www.ingramcontent.com/pod-product-compliance
Lightning Source LLC
Chambersburg PA
CBHW032158190726
48289CB00007BA/2290